PAWSITIVELY LOVE

A SWEET SINGLE MOM ROMANCE

CHRISTIE LOGAN

D1304755

This book is dedicated to the memory of Denise C., a wonderful writer, critique partner, and friend, who knew a lot about Good Dogs.

CHAPTER 1

Harley

I am a Bad Dog.

"Bad dog, Harley!" My people shouted when I sneaked out of my yard to visit my cat friend next door. I only wanted to play.

"Bad boy!" When I barked at that man who came to our house every day and left papers in the little box near our door. Didn't my family understand I was protecting them?

And that time someone left a yummy steak on the counter? I tried so hard to leave it alone, but its delicious smell tickled and teased my poor nose. It made my mouth water and my hungry tummy grumble. I only meant to take a little nibble, but it tasted so good...

"Bad dog! Bad!"

That must be why my people left me here, in a cage in this big room. All the dogs here are in cages. Are they bad, too?

I miss my family so much it hurts my heart. Won't they ever come back for me? If they only would, I promise I'd be good forever and ever.

The door to the big room opens and I hear footsteps.

Some of the dogs bark loud at the sound. Some whine and cry. Some lie sadly and hopelessly, knowing their families are never coming back.

I don't move as the footsteps near my cage. When I first came here, I'd jump to my paws every time the door opened, hoping my people had come back for me. I don't do that anymore. I don't think I'll ever see my family again.

"What's wrong, Harley?" A familiar voice asks. It's Walter, the man who brings my breakfast and supper every day. He's nice, so I wag my tail for him a tiny bit, even though I'm very sad.

"I'm worried about you, pal," he says. "You didn't finish your breakfast today."

I wasn't very hungry. It's hard to eat when your heart hurts so bad. But I don't want him to worry, so I pad to the door of my cage and let him skritch my head through the wire opening. It feels good.

"Don't be so downhearted, buddy," he tells me. "It's a big day. Adoption Day here at the shelter. Lots of people will be coming through, looking for pets. You gotta show your stuff. You know, make a good impression. Maybe someone will take you home, too."

He gives me another skritch and my tail wags a little more. *Home.* The word makes me happy inside. If only I could go home again.

"That's right, Harl. Somebody's sure to want a good dog like you."

My tail droops and so do my ears. Nobody will want me. Because I am not a good dog. I am Bad. Why else would my family leave me here?

I lie in my corner as people come and go. They are all different shapes, sizes, and colors—just like us dogs. Some are tall, some are small. Some are round, some are thin. Some come alone, others are in pairs, and some are grown-ups with little kids. They stop and look at us, talk to us. When they stop at my cage, I wag my tail a bit just to be polite. But I don't lift my head or stand up eagerly to greet them, like some of the other dogs do. These people are nice, but they are not *my* people.

Two new people stop by my cage. A grown-up lady and a little girl. "What does it say, Mom?"

The little girl's voice tickles something in my brain and my ears perk up. I raise my head and look at her. She has yellow fur on her head, a funny hat with pointy things on it, and a friendly smile. I think I've seen her before. I've smelled her before, too. She smells like milk and maple syrup and soap and sunshine.

She smells nice.

The lady named Mom has yellow fur on her head, just like the little girl. She smells good, too. She reads the card on the outside of my cage. "It says his name is Harley. Honey, he's too big. Remember, we're looking for a small dog." She tries to hurry them along, but the little girl doesn't move.

"What else does the card say? Why is he here?"

I lower my head. Now they will find out I am Bad. I don't want that. I want them to like me.

The lady sighs. "It says here he kept running away from home. That's why the people who owned him brought him here."

I let out a whimper. That's not true. I never ran away. I only sneaked out of the yard to play with my neighbor cat. I never went far.

The little girl's smile fades but her eyes are kind. "If he ran away, I bet they were mean to him."

"Gracie, we don't know that. Anyway, come on. There are more dogs to see."

Gracie. That name tickles my brain again and I give a loud woof. Now I remember!

She remembers, too. "Mommy, this is the dog we met at that lady's house. Aunt Shelley's friend. When we went swimming in her pool, remember? He came over and wanted to play with us. It's Harley!"

Gracie's face breaks into a big smile. I smile too and hurry to the cage door to greet her. Yes, I met her that day at my neighbor cat's house. She wore the same hat with pointy things and booped me on the head with a sparkly stick.

"You're a good dog," she told me.

Maybe I *could* be Good, with her.

"Gracie," the lady says. But Gracie doesn't move. We look into each other's eyes and know we are friends.

"I like *him*, Mom," she says. "I like Harley."

She pokes her fingers through the wire and pets my nose. My heart is a happy bouncy ball and my tail goes round and round in joy. When I lick her fingers, she giggles.

"Don't do that," the lady says, pulling her back. "Be careful."

Is she afraid I'll bite? I would never hurt Gracie.

Gracie knows that, too. "It tickles, Mom. Look at his tail. It looks just like a pinwheel. He wants to go home with us. Please, can't we adopt him?"

Please, Mom? I want to go home with Gracie. She is my friend. I love her.

Please say yes.

CHAPTER 2

Savannah

"Please, Mom? Can't we take Harley home? Please?"

Savannah Kaminski steeled herself as Gracie turned big pleading eyes her way. It wasn't as though she'd never told her daughter "No" before. Since she was a mom, the word was a tried-and-true part of her vocabulary:

"No, Gracie, you can't have cupcakes for breakfast."

"No, you can't stay up and watch another show. It's bedtime."

"I don't care how hot it is, you can't wear your bathing suit to school. No."

But all those noes were for her daughter's own good. It hurt to refuse her something she wanted so badly. Something that, under other circumstances, Savannah would have been happy to grant her.

Savannah's heart twisted. *Here it comes. The tsunami of guilt in three...two...one...*

"No, honey. I'm sorry. We can't take him home."

Gracie's chin quivered. Her lower lip pooched out and tears swam in her eyes. Savannah knew her daughter well enough to recognize when she was practicing for an Academy Award and when she was truly upset. These tears were real.

"But why, Mom? Why can't we?"

"He's too big. We said we were going to get a little dog, remember?"

As Gracie's mouth drooped even more, the big Black Labrador Retriever let out a whimper and gazed up at Savannah pleadingly. Great, now she had *two* pairs of sad puppy eyes to contend with.

Stay strong, she told herself. Gently placing her hands on Gracie's shoulders, she tried to steer her away from the big dog's cage. "Come on, now. He's a nice dog, but there are plenty of nice dogs here. Let's go find one that's right for us."

But Gracie curled her fingers in the cage's wire, refusing to budge. "I don't want another dog. I want Harley."

"We can't. Mr. and Mrs. Russo won't let us bring a big dog home." It had been hard enough convincing their landlords to allow them a small dog. Luckily, they had a soft spot for Gracie and were willing to bend the rules when they learned how desperately she wanted a pet.

"We can talk to them, Mom," her daughter answered, her face alight with hope. "We'll tell them Harley will be a good watchdog."

Harley gave a small woof at that, prancing in his cage as though to say *"Yes! Just let me show my stuff."*

Holding onto her patience by a thread, Savannah tried a different tack. "It wouldn't be fair to Harley, though. Look at what a big boy he is. He needs a house and a yard to run around in. He'll have lots of energy and need to go out for long walks every day." Not to mention all the food he'd eat. How much strain would that put on their already tight budget?

"I'll walk him, Mom."

"He's too big for you to handle. And we only have a small apartment. There's barely enough room for us and Aunt Shelley." Savannah's younger sister was staying with them after suffering some financial setbacks.

"That's all right. He can sleep with me. And Aunt Shelley can help. She knows a lot about dogs."

It was all Savannah could do not to roll her eyes. For every challenge she posed, Gracie had an answer. They might stand here all day, arguing back and forth. Time to stop being reasonable and pull out the mother of all momisms: *"Because I said so."*

"No, Gracie. No more discussion. Now, come." Her voice came out more harshly than she intended. The disappointment on her daughter's face wrecked her. It hurt every time she had to refuse her little girl something she really wanted. Gracie already missed so much, not having a dad in her life. Why shouldn't she have a dog? A big dog, if she wanted, one to hug and chase around and play with? Why shouldn't Harley have a home with a loving little girl to care for and protect?

But Savannah had to be sensible. How could she care for Harley—and she *knew* most of the care would fall to her, in spite of Gracie's good intentions—when she had a fulltime job, a young child to raise, *and* the coursework she needed to finish to obtain her master's degree? She was already stretched to the limit. There was no way she could handle the extra work and expense a dog like this would surely entail.

Gracie's expression went from sad to stubborn. She firmed her small mouth and shook her head, her hands glued to the wire of Harley's cage. "No. I don't want any other dog. I want Harley."

Harley, seeming to pick up on the impasse, licked Gracie's fingers and whined pathetically. Planting his bottom on the concrete floor, he stared at Savannah anxiously. His big brown eyes seemed to beg *"Can't you help us? Can't you do something?"*

"I can't," she wanted to tell him. *"I'm already torn in two."*

A voice broke through the tense moment. "Are you interested in Harley?"

A man approached them, wearing a big smile. He wore a blue shirt that seemed to be the uniform for all the employees of the Happy Hearts Animal Shelter. On the shirt pocket was a pin that said *Walter*.

"He's a nice dog," Walter went on. "Make some family a real good pet. Huh, wouldn't you, boy?"

Harley woofed and pranced as though saying *"You bet! Just give me a chance!"*

Walter laughed. "Yeah, that's right. You tell 'em."

"I'm afraid he's too big for us," Savannah answered, not wanting to give Gracie any false hope.

"Aw, that's too bad. It's harder to place the big dogs. People think they're too much work."

Guilt stung Savannah as Gracie gave her an accusatory look. "He seems friendly enough. I'm sure someone will give him a good home."

"I sure hope so." Walter sighed. "He's got a lot of love to give."

"The card says he ran away a lot. That's why his people surrendered him."

The man shrugged. "People give all kinds of excuses when they bring pets here. Sometimes they're legitimate, sometimes..." he shrugged and let the sentence trail off unfinished.

Gracie's forehead crinkled. "What's legitament? What's that mean?"

"Legitimate. It means real. Truthful," Savannah answered.

"You mean maybe they lied about him? Maybe he didn't run away?" Gracie looked at Walter, then back at her mom.

Savannah responded with a tired sigh. "Gracie, it really doesn't matter anyway. Harley's a nice dog, but we simply cannot take him."

"That's a shame," Walter said. "He's been pretty depressed since he landed here. People say animals don't have feelings. That's not true. I've seen a lot of broken-hearted pets in my time here. They know they've been left behind."

At that, Gracie's chin quivered. "Poor Harley," she whispered. The big dog whimpered and pushed his nose against the wire door, urging her to pet him.

"I'm sure he'd bounce right back though, if he had a family to love," Walter went on, oblivious to the guilt twisting in Savannah's chest.

She gave him a surreptitious glare. *Thanks a lot, dude. Way to make me this even harder. Do you think I enjoy breaking my daughter's heart?*

Then, glancing at Harley, she amended the thought. *Make that two hearts.*

Just when Savannah thought it couldn't get worse, Gracie gazed up at her, a plea in her eyes. "You see, Mom? Harley *needs* us. He needs us to love him. And we need him."

Savannah took a deep breath, gathering her strength in preparation to issue that final *no*. Preparing for the deluge of tears that were sure to follow.

Some of those tears would be hers. She'd be breaking three hearts today, including her own.

CHAPTER 3

Drew

Drew Woodson wasn't looking to adopt a pet. He wasn't sure what made him step into the dog area of the Happy Hearts Animal Shelter. Maybe it was curiosity, or nostalgia for the fond memories he had of the dog who'd been his best boyhood pal. Once inside, he expected to hear plenty of excited woofs, yips, and growls. What he didn't expect to find was a little girl in tears. And beside her, a woman who looked like she wanted to burst out crying herself.

A guy, one of the workers there, turned to him. "Did you need some help, sir?"

"No, not really," he answered, shrugging. "Just wanted to, uh, look around."

As he spoke, his gaze kept drifting to the little girl. He hated to see a kid cry.

The woman with her, who had to be her mom, spoke quietly. "Gracie, I've explained more than once. If you can't cooperate, we're just going to have to go home."

"I don't care," the child wept. "I don't want any other dog. I only want Harley."

The worker—Walter, according to his name tag—looked a bit embarrassed by the scene. "Okay, sir. We have lots of nice dogs here." He tried to hustle Drew along in another direction, away from the mother and child. "Feel free to look around."

"Thanks," he murmured, focusing on the little girl. Geez, she was crying her heart out. Kids got so emotional over animals. Drew swallowed a lump in his throat, remembering how much he'd loved Boomer, the big clumsy Golden Retriever he'd had as a kid.

Instead of letting Walter lead him away, Drew found himself moving toward Gracie and her mother, near the cage holding the Black Lab. Gesturing to the dog, he said "Who's this fella right here?"

Anger sparked in the little girl's eyes and she poked out her chin stubbornly. "Leave him alone."

The mom gave a shocked gasp. "Gracie. Don't be rude."

Drew wasn't offended. He kind of admired the kid's spunk. Hoping to stem her flow of tears, he crouched to Gracie's level and gestured to the bedazzled plastic crown on her head. "What are you, a princess or something? I've never talked to a princess before."

She gave him a shy smile. "No, silly. I'm a fairy."

"Oh, of course. I should have guessed. Are you going to cast a spell?"

Brushing away tears, she shook her head. "I don't have my magic wand."

"But fairies don't need wands to do magic. Oops, I shouldn't have said that. You might put a spell on me." He pretended to shiver and shake. "Oh, please, Ms. Fairy, don't turn me into a frog."

She giggled and touched her finger to his forehead. "Boop. You're a frog."

Drew began to croak. "Ribbit. Ribbit."

They both dissolved into laughter while Gracie's mom looked on, a smile blooming across her face. She was lovely when she smiled. Drew's chest swelled with pride for helping these two ladies forget their sadness, if only for a moment.

Walter cleared his throat. "Maybe you'd like to take Harley out for a bit. We're hosting the Waggle Walk today to raise money for a new building."

Harley woofed and pranced, as though saying *Yes! Please let me out!*

Drew stood. He hadn't planned on taking part in the walkathon, just as he hadn't planned to look step inside the dog enclosure. But now that he was here, Harley's enthusiasm and friendliness touched him, reminding him of Boomer.

Glancing down at Gracie, he said "What do you think? It would be nice for him to get out of his cage for a while."

But Gracie still looked uncertain.

"It's for a real good cause," Drew went on, using his most persuasive tone. He knew how to seal a deal. "This special day will raise money to help a lot of animals."

Gracie bit her lip, then nodded. "My Aunt Shelley helps animals. She works at the vet clinic."

"Your aunt?" The name rang a bell. "Is that Shelley Kaminski?"

Gracie nodded, her eyes round. "Do you know her?"

"I've met her. She's my friend Ty's...uh..."

Her eyes popped rounder. "His girlfriend! Mommy, he knows Aunt Shelley. And Ty. Ty's my tee ball coach!" She looked amazed at what she considered an extraordinary coincidence.

"You play tee ball? That's awesome. Ty's my good friend. We used to be teammates, as a matter of fact."

Ty Garrett had moved upstate to Verona Lake after retiring from the major leagues, becoming something of a local celebrity. His presence helped bring some attention to good causes, like this one, in the lakeside community. Since Drew was already in town, he'd shown up today to support his friend's cause.

Their conversation was interrupted by a loud woof from Harley, who tilted his head and looked at them as though saying *"Hey, what's going on? Did you forget about me, or what?"*

Drew laughed. "Yeah, I think this guy really wants out."

"Let me get a leash for him," Walter said. "I'll be right back."

"You're only going to borrow him, right?" Gracie asked. "You're not going to keep Harley, are you?"

"Don't talk like that," her mother said. "You should want Harley to get a good home."

The little girl's chin jutted stubbornly. "But he needs to live with *us!*"

"Here's a thought." The words escaped Drew's mouth before the idea fully formed in his brain. "Maybe you and your mom can join Harley and me on the Waggle Walk."

Dude, what are you even doing? A voice in his head sounded. *You came here today to shake a few hands, make a nice donation, then split. The plan is to lie low here in town, right? So why get chummy with this kid and her mom? And a dog on top of it?*

He ignored the scolding voice. He wanted to make this little girl happy. Was that a crime? He wanted to smooth the worries from her mother's face and see that pretty smile again. If he could do that by taking a goofy dog for a walk, so be it.

Hope filled Gracie's face, chasing away her tears. "Can we, Mom? Can we, please?"

The woman flashed him a narrow look that said, *"Thanks a lot, mister,"* and Drew realized his gaffe. He should have cleared the plan with Mom before opening his big mouth and inserting his foot up to the knee. Now he'd put her on the spot. If she said no, she'd be the bad guy.

"Please?" Gracie begged. Harley chimed in with a pathetic whine.

With a sigh of surrender, the woman nodded. Her smile looked forced. "All right. For a little while. But no tantrums when it's time to say goodbye."

"I promise," Gracie said, hopping with excitement.

The woman's smile fell away when Drew sent her an apologetic look. He could have kicked himself. *Way to make a good impression.*

At least he'd won Gracie over. She watched in fascination as Walter returned and entered Harley's cage to put a collar and leash on him.

"Can I hold him?" she asked when the employee led the dog out of his enclosure.

"He's big boy and he looks pretty strong," Drew answered, taking the leash. "You better let me do it."

Her disappointment lasted only a moment, because Harley eagerly licked her hand, making her giggle. She threw her arms around the dog's neck and he pressed against her, his whole body one big, excited wiggle. "He likes me."

Drew grinned. "He sure does."

Gracie's mom wasn't smiling. Her face had settled into a look of resignation.

Time to smooth things over with her as best he could. Holding Harley's leash in his left hand, he offered his right. "I'm Drew Woodson."

The woman hesitated, then briefly shook his hand. Drew found himself reluctant to end the contact. "Savannah Kaminski."

If no smile accompanied her introduction, at least he knew her name. It was a start.

CHAPTER 4

Savannah

They strolled through the crispy fallen leaves on the course along with other dogs and their owners. Savannah tried to keep a close eye on Gracie, who walked at Harley's side. But more than once, she found her gaze slipping to Drew Woodson. He certainly was easy on the eyes.

"This is real nice event," he said. "It's a shame your husband couldn't join you and Gracie today."

Savannah slid him a glance and found her gaze lingering. He wasn't movie-star handsome, but his dark eyes and the dimple in his chin made his face arresting. His expression was innocent—bland, even. Was he simply making an offhand comment, or fishing to find out if she was married?

Get over yourself, girlfriend. It's a simple remark. Don't be one of those desperate chicks who thinks any man who makes conversation is interested in you.

She answered in the same casual way he'd spoken. "There's no husband. It's just me and my daughter."

"Oh. Sorry."

"Don't be," she replied, a bit too sharp. "Grace and I do just fine."

Oh, great. Snap his head off. That's a perfect way to show how well you're doing.

"I'm sure you do." He answered smoothly, letting her snark bounce right off him, which only sharpened the bite of guilt.

Most days Savannah figured she had the single mom thing down pat. Not that she had much time to rest on her laurels—her days were a whirlwind from the moment she woke up to the minute she laid her head on her pillow at bedtime. Up at six every morning, shower and dress, wake Gracie and help her get ready for school. Breakfast. Pack lunches for them both. And of course, the last-minute scramble for permission slips that needed signing, books due back to the school library, the search for some item that Gracie simply *had to* have.

By the time she arrived at school with Gracie, Savannah was ready for a nap. Instead, she had to face down a roomful of fourth graders. She loved her students, but who else besides a teacher was required to be a combination cheer-leader, entertainer, counselor, and disciplinarian all at once? She barely had a moment to breathe, much less sit down.

After school there was paperwork, preparations, and meetings. Then it was time to grab Gracie from her after-school program and race home. Snack. Homework. Dinner. Clean up, then more paperwork for Savannah while Gracie enjoyed a bit of screen time before bed. Then of course the nightly wrangling with her daughter: "But the show's not over. Can't I stay up a little while longer? *Please?* Aw, no fair."

After her daughter was in bed, Savannah made corrections until the words on the papers melted into blurs before her bleary eyes. Bed by eleven, if she was lucky.

Then the whole thing started again.

Big whoop. Your life's no different than any other working mom's. But those moms, at least many of them, had a partner. Someone to share the burdens and responsibilities. Someone who might say "You look wiped, baby. Let me fix dinner tonight." Or "Since you cooked tonight, I'll clean up. Why don't you put your feet up for a couple minutes?"

Someone who'd toss a load of laundry into the washing machine while you cleared the dishes and wiped down the table. Someone whose strong fingers would massage the kinks from your neck and shoulders. Someone who'd collapse next to you on the sofa and take your hand. There'd be no need for words. You'd simply exchange weary, grateful smiles.

We made it through another day. Together.

It was a lovely dream. One Savannah didn't allow herself to indulge in much. But days like this, she felt down on herself. Not so much for what she was missing—she was an adult and could handle it. But she felt sad for Gracie, not having a dad in her life.

None of that was Drew Woodson's fault. *The man's trying to be nice, going out of his way for your daughter's sake, and the first thing you do is jump down his throat.*

He handled the dog easily, with confidence. Harley, big and full of energy, tugged at the leash as though he wanted to speed up, but Drew controlled the pace. His hands were large and strong.

A flash of warmth rolled from her collar to her face, heating her cheeks. *For gosh sakes, Savannah. You act like you've never seen a man before.*

To distract herself, and in way of an apology, she said "You really seem to know what you're doing," indicating his hold on the leash.

He seemed pleased by her compliment. "Do I? Maybe I haven't lost my touch, then."

That piqued her interest. "Have you had a lot of experience with dogs?"

He hesitated. "I haven't owned a dog in a long time. When I was with the Condors, I was away from home so often it didn't make sense to have one. And when I left the game and got into my next gig, the hours were so long, it wouldn't have been fair. Dogs need companionship. When I was a kid, though, yeah. I had a big Golden Retriever named Boomer." He gave a laugh. "Man, that dog was crazy. Totally lived up to his name, booming around, getting into everything. I spent a lot of time trying to keep him out of trouble, training him. He turned out to be a real good dog, though." Drew's expression grew thoughtful. "He really got me through."

Through what? she wondered. Of course, she didn't voice the question.

"Well, you certainly make it look easy," she commented. "I think this guy would knock me off my feet if I was holding the leash."

"He's been cooped up in that cage for who knows how long. It's natural he'd be a bit hyper. But the exercise is good for him. Helps him work off the energy. He's starting to calm down a little. See how he keeps looking over to Gracie, like he's checking to see she's still there? I think he's found a friend."

From the looks of it, Gracie felt the same way. She was chatting away with Harley as though they were already best buds. Savannah sighed as guilt descended once again. Maybe it had been a mistake to agree to this walk. The more time they spent with the dog, the harder it would be to say goodbye at the end of the day. There were sure to be more tears.

"You know, with some training, I think Harley could make someone a real nice pet."

She slid him a sidelong glance. "Someone like Gracie, you mean?"

He shrugged. "Could be."

His blasé act didn't fool her at all. A hot spurt of anger shot through her. Lowering her voice, she said "Do you think I enjoy telling my daughter no? Disappointing her when I know she's got her heart set on something?"

"Of course not," he answered quickly, his expression turning apologetic. "I only meant—"

She cut him off. "Please. I understand you mean well, but you don't know my life."

He nodded. "You're right."

"An animal this size would be expensive to feed. He'd need a lot of room. A yard to run and play in. I live in two-bedroom apartment." She'd gone through it all with Gracie. Why was she explaining to him? He didn't care. It was none of his business, anyway.

Still, she couldn't stop herself. "Don't you see? It wouldn't be fair." She wasn't some hard-hearted ogre. She was just a mom trying to keep a lot of balls in the air. Trying to make life for herself and her daughter...who, at that very moment, was about to give Harley a drink from her water bottle.

"Gracie, no!"

"But he's thirsty, Mom. His tongue is hanging out."

"If he's thirsty, we'll get him some water. Do *not* let him drink from your bottle."

"There's a station right there," Drew said, indicating one of the spots along the route where volunteers had bowls of water ready for thirsty pups and bottled water for people walking them. "We can take a little break, too." He glanced at Gracie. "What do you say, Ms. Fairy?"

She smiled, enjoying his attention. "I say, good."

They sat on a bench in the shade under a tall tree, sipping water while Harley lapped up two bowls full.

"See, Mom? I told you he was thirsty," Gracie said. Harley raised his head and gave them a big doggy grin. Then he shook his head, spraying Gracie with water from his wet muzzle. "Yah! He got me all wet!"

Alarm shot through Savannah, but Drew just laughed. "That means he likes you." As though to convince her of that, the dog trotted over and licked Gracie's hand. She giggled and scratched his head. Harley apparently could do no wrong.

Drew gave him a playful noogie between the ears. "He's a clown, isn't he? Makes me think of my guy Boomer."

Gracie's eyes went wide. "You have a dog?"

"Well, he's not around anymore. Had him when I was a kid. He'd do all kinds of silly things."

"Like what?"

"Well, I remember once on my birthday, my mom made this really nice cake for me. She put it on the counter and went to do something else for a minute, and Boomer snuck into the kitchen. He was a big dog—a Golden Retriever, you know what they are?—and when my mom wasn't looking, he stood up on his hind legs and took a big bite—"

Gracie gasped, then giggled. "Did he eat the whole thing?"

"It was half-gone by the time Mom caught him. She yelled and he ran out of the room like his tail was on fire."

"What did you do then?"

Drew shrugged. "Well, we still had half a cake."

Gracie's face twisted in disbelieving horror. "You *ate* it?"

"Sure. It was my birthday. We just cut off the parts the dog slobbered on and ate the rest. It tasted fine."

Savannah chuckled, drawn into the story as well.

"Did Boomer get in trouble?" her daughter asked.

"He knew Mom was mad at him, so he made himself scarce and hid out in my bedroom. She got even madder though when she got up the next morning and found a big pile of dog barf in the hallway. I guess the cake didn't agree with him."

Gracie's nose wrinkled in disgust. "Eww. Nasty. What else did Boomer do?"

Drew scratched his chin in thought. Harley sighed as though bored by these stories of a dog he'd never met. He lay down on the cool grass.

"Well, there was this dog that lived down the street. A big German Shepherd mix. What was his name again? Oh, yeah. Sparky."

"Was he mean?"

"No, no. He was a nice dog. Friendly and all that. When I took Boomer out for walks, Sparky would always run to the edge of the fence and stick his nose through. Like he wanted to be friends, you know? Anyway, one day Sparky got out of his yard and came up to our house. We had a back porch with a rickety old screen door. Boomer was on the porch that day and when he saw Sparky, he busted right through the screen to get at him."

"Did they fight?"

"No, they were playing. Chasing each other around the yard, running and jumping. Thing was my mom had a bunch of laundry hanging on the clothesline. And these two guys, they were just so wild that they ended up knocking down the line and getting all tangled up in it. Dragging the clothes on the ground and getting them all dirty." He shook his head. "Man, was that a mess. When we finally untangled the dogs and got Sparky home, we had to wash the clothes all over again."

"I bet your mom was mad."

"Oh, she was steaming. But she never stayed mad long." Drew smiled. "She loved Boomer as much as I did."

"What about your dad? Did he love Boomer, too?"

Drew hesitated. "Uh… no. I mean, my dad wasn't part of my life then."

Gracie's face grew serious, and she nodded as though she knew exactly where he was coming from. "Yeah. I don't have a dad, either."

An invisible fist squeezed Savannah's heart, making her catch her breath. She never wanted it to be this way. She'd grown up without a father and had felt that loss firsthand. She'd never wanted to put her own child in that position.

And yet, despite all her good intentions, she'd done exactly that.

Distracted by these thoughts, she didn't immediately notice a little girl toddling past holding her father's hand. In her other hand was an ice cream cone.

Harley leaped to his feet, straining at the leash to sniff out the treat. The child, startled, bumped against her father and dropped the cone onto the grass. Harley gobbled the ice cream treat in two bites.

The little girl burst into tears. Her dad scooped her up into his arms and glared at Drew. "See what that mutt did? Why aren't you watching him?"

"Harley, sit," Drew commanded sharply. Harley, who seemed to know he'd messed up, immediately planted his butt on the ground. Then, after passing the leash to Savannah, Drew stood and approached the angry man.

"Hey, you're right. Totally my bad. I should have kept a better eye on him."

The man blinked in surprise, as though he'd expected a confrontation instead of an apology. Some of the anger left his face. "Yeah, well…" he patted his daughter's back as she hid her face against his shoulder. "He scared her, you know?"

"I am so sorry about that." Drew pulled his wallet from his pocket and took out a ten-dollar bill. "Do me a favor, huh? Take this and buy your little girl another ice cream. Get yourself one, too."

The other man hesitated, peering at Drew. "Hey, aren't you..."

"Drew Woodson," Drew answered with a big grin. "Yeah, you got me. How you doin'?"

"Good. Good. Hey, nice to meet you. I'm a big Condors fan. Uh, why'd you quit the game when you were still going strong?"

Drew's grin didn't slip. "Well, you know what they say about getting out while you're still on top."

"You got that TV thing going on now, right? I've caught it a few times. Good show."

"Thanks, man. I really appreciate that."

The man glanced at the bill Drew held. "You don't need to do that."

"I insist. Please. It'll make me feel better." He pressed the money into the man's hand and smiled at the little girl peeking at him from her father's shoulder. "Did the doggie scare you, honey? I'm sorry."

Gracie spoke up. "He's not mean. He just wanted a lick of your ice cream cone. He didn't mean to make you drop it."

"She's okay." The man patted his daughter's back. "Aren't you, Manda?"

"His name's Harley," Gracie added. "He's nice. Want to pet him?"

Harley's tail swept back and forth. Savannah tightened her grip on his leash, not knowing how the dog would react. "Gracie."

"It's okay, Mom. He'll be good," she answered innocently.

Savannah didn't share her confidence.

"What do you say, honey?" Manda's dad gently set her down. "Want to pet him?"

Manda nodded shyly. Holding her father's hand, she

toddled over to Harley, who lifted his head as though he wanted to sniff her.

The little girl shrank back.

"It's okay," Gracie said softly. "Like this." She stroked Harley between the ears. "See?"

Savannah tensed as her hold tautened on the dog's leash. She didn't think he'd bite, but he didn't know his own strength. She didn't want him leaping in excitement and knocking Manda down.

The little girl approached again and petted Harley as Gracie had shown her. Thankfully, he stayed sitting. Only his tail moved, whapping back and forth in delight. Manda giggled when the dog's tongue curled out and licked her fingers.

"See? He likes that," Gracie said.

Smiling, Manda stroked him and looked up at her father. "Daddy!"

"I see, honey." Her dad leaned down and gave Harley a pat. The dog's hind end waggled but otherwise he stayed still.

"Good boy," Savannah murmured, giving a silent sigh of relief.

"Come on, Manda," her father said. "Let's go get that ice cream." He turned to Drew. "Thanks, man. Nice meeting you."

"Same here."

As Manda and her dad walked away, Drew and Gracie exchanged smiles, as though they were a team. And maybe they had been, working together to get Harley out of trouble.

Pride warmed Savannah at the way Gracie had encouraged little Manda to overcome her fear. She'd been so calm and sure of herself, acting almost like a big sister. How amazing. As well as Savannah knew her daughter, Gracie still had the ability to surprise her.

And this Drew Woodson. Though she hated to admit it,

something about him fascinated her. He seemed to have the magic touch.

He'd jollied Gracie out of her tears. He'd gotten Harley to sit and behave, if only briefly. Faced with an angry guy who might have gladly punched him out, Drew talked him down until they parted practically friends.

How does he do it? How does he make it all look so easy?

What she'd give for some of his confidence. She spent so much time feeling frazzled, one step away from completely fried. How she'd love to sail through life with that ease and assurance, knowing every obstacle would fall in the face of her charm.

Not so fast. What about that other charmer you fell for? Remember him?

Gracie's father. Like a magician, he'd woven a spell around her. Literally charmed the pants off her. And when she learned she was pregnant…poof. He disappeared in a puff of smoke.

Come on, now. You can't put it all on him. You went along very willingly.

True. It was easy to cast herself in the role of victim, but she could have said no any step of the way. Could have kept her head on straight, not fallen for his blandishments and lies.

She'd wanted to believe he really loved her.

Fool me once, shame on you. Fool me twice…

No. She would not play the fool twice. She would never fall for another charmer.

CHAPTER 5

Drew

He had a much easier time befriending Gracie than winning over the lovely Savannah. Though the woman relaxed a bit as the three of them—four, if you counted Harley—spent the next couple of hours together, it wasn't easy getting to know her. An invisible wall surrounded her. She was perfectly polite, but distant, never letting him too close. As though to protect herself.

Gracie was a different story. She was a cute little thing and smart, too. She'd really impressed him, the way she'd stepped up to defend Harley after his mishap with Manda. Not to mention how she'd befriended the child, helping her overcome her fear of the dog. He and Gracie had been a team, working to win over the frightened child and angry dad.

And Harley, despite his over-enthusiasm, had a charm all his own. Though the dog needed plenty of training and discipline, Drew had the sense that he wanted to please people. His natural exuberance just got in the way.

After they finished the walkathon, Drew bought them ice

creams. The same vendor even sold dog-friendly frozen treats, so Harley did not miss out. Then they poked around some of the nearby stalls where vendors sold pet accessories and other items.

When he'd first arrived at the pet adoption event, he'd planned to stay only briefly and make a hasty exit. Now, as the day wound down, he was sorry to see it end.

"Gracie, I think it's time we should be going." Savannah's comment to her daughter struck a dismal chord with Drew.

Gracie's expression collapsed in sadness. "Do we have to?"

"Yes, honey. Harley needs to get his supper. And we're going out for pizza with Aunt Shelley. Remember?" Though Savannah's tone was even-tempered, the crease in her forehead and the tightness of her lips showed her strain.

The little girl hugged Harley around the neck. "Harley doesn't want to say goodbye. He wants to stay with me."

Harley whimpered as though to say, *"Yes, I do."*

"*You* just don't like him," Gracie muttered. "You're mean."

"That's not true," Drew heard himself say. "Don't talk to your mom that way."

Savannah's eyes shot him a warning that said, *"I don't need your help."*

Yeah, he'd overstepped. But Gracie couldn't see that her mom was hurting, too.

Of course, she can't see. She's just a kid. A kid too in love with a dog to see anything.

Oh, man. She was crying again, burying her face in Harley's fur. He couldn't handle it. Even as a kid, it killed him when his little sister Adrienne cried. To stop the tears, he'd take her stuffed elephant Miss Elly and pretend it was talking to her. He'd used a funny voice and say silly things to make her giggle. Her laughter always made him feel like a million bucks.

He wished he could think of something funny now. He never should have gotten involved in this deal. He'd thought he could help, but all he'd done was delay the eventual heartbreak.

"I do like Harley." Savannah answered her daughter calmly. "He's rambunctious, but I don't think he means any harm. But we can't take him, Gracie. For all the reasons we discussed. Mr. Russo won't let us get a dog that big."

"I don't like Mr. Russo," Gracie said darkly. "He's mean."

"Don't say that. You know it's not true. He's been very kind to us." Savannah took a deep breath. "They're closing up here, but I tell you what—we'll come back next Saturday and—"

Gracie's mulishness vanished. She lit up with hope. "And visit Harley?"

"And we'll look for a smaller dog that we can bring home," Savannah finished.

"But what about Harley? What if he's gone by then? Somebody else might take him away."

"Don't you want him to find a good home?"

"*We're* a good home." Gracie wept as though her heart were being torn in two. Maybe it was. She loved that dog the way only a child could. "I don't *want* to tell Harley goodbye."

Drew found himself blinking hard. Man, those tears were ripping him apart. "Maybe you don't have to say goodbye."

Had he really said that? Yes, he must have, because Gracie gaped at him in awe.

Savannah's narrowed eyes were lasers. *What are you doing?* She glared as though she wanted to throttle him.

What are you doing? A voice in his brain echoed. *Dude, you've lost it.*

Whatever. He couldn't stand to see Gracie hurting.

Well, think fast, genius. You had to open your big mouth. What are you gonna do now?

"Maybe somebody could volunteer to foster Harley…" He'd seen the sign inside the building: *Would you like to foster a pet?* "You know, take him home and teach him how to behave himself. And you could visit him whenever you wanted—maybe even help out…"

Gracie's eyes popped wide. "I could?"

"And who would this marvelous 'somebody' be?" Savannah's voice was silky, her expression grim.

Yeah, you're in it, aren't you buddy? Right up to your neck. So go big or go home.

"Me," he answered.

CHAPTER 6

Drew

Gracie stared at him in wonder. "Really?"

Savannah looked like she wanted to dropkick him. "Gracie, it looks like Aunt Shelley's arrived." Drew recognized Shelley right away. In fact, he'd been instrumental in matching her up with his friend Ty. "See? She's over by that stand selling dog and cat collars. Go on over and say hi."

"Can I take Harley with me?"

"Harley can stay here a minute. You go see Aunt Shelley. I want to talk to Mr. Woodson."

Dum da dum dum. The warning notes of the *Dragnet* theme sounded in Drew's head. He was in for a scolding, at the very least.

Savannah remained quiet until her daughter was out of earshot. Then, pinning Drew with an icy glare, she said "What do you think you're doing?"

What did she want him to say? "Just what I plan to do—"

"How can you raise my daughter's hopes like that and string her along with false promises—"

That stung. His offer may have been impulsive, but in no

way was it false. "Hold on. I don't lie and when I make a promise, I keep my word. Stringing her along? I'd never do that to anyone, much less a kid."

Savannah gave a huff of disbelief. "You don't even live in town. Do you think you can bring the dog to some hotel room?"

"I am living here. I'm renting a house on the lake, not far from Ty's." This town seemed like the perfect spot to fly under the radar for a bit and Ty had hooked him up with a local real estate agent. Drew was renting a place whose owner was spending the next few months touring Europe.

"For how long? A few weeks? What happens when you've tired of this sudden whim? Does Harley go back to the shelter? And what about Gracie? Do you just break her heart?"

Now he was mad. This woman was determined to make him out a thoughtless clod who cared nothing about hurting a dog and a little girl. "Absolutely not. This is the real deal. I'm going to foster Harley and train him to be a good dog."

Harley whimpered. He looked from Savannah to Drew with frightened eyes that seemed to ask *"Why are you fighting?"*

Drew rubbed the dog's head. "It's okay, guy."

If he had any doubts before, the trust in Harley's big brown eyes knocked them clean out of him. By gosh, he *was* going to do it. He'd prove he could be trusted. That he cared.

Glancing back at Savannah, he said "I hope you'll let Gracie come visit him once in a while."

Some of the suspicion left her face and she looked as if she wanted to believe him but didn't dare. "Why would you do this?"

He didn't need to stop and think to answer her. "Because I know how it feels to be a kid and love an animal. And I know how much it hurts to say goodbye."

Savannah's eyes flew wide. She sucked in a sharp breath.

"Gracie doesn't feel that way about Harley. It's only been a few hours."

"That's plenty of time to fall in love."

She shook her head as if she didn't know what to say.

Gracie appeared with her Aunt Shelley. It was easy to see the resemblance between Savannah and her sister, though Shelley was a bit shorter and quicker to smile. She wore a big grin as she stroked Harley's ears. "Hey, there! I remember you. Wondered where you went. How'd you end up here, guy?"

"His people gave him away," Gracie answered. "But that's okay because Mr. Woodson is going to take him home. And he said I could come visit Harley and help train him, even."

"Oh, really?" Shelley gave her sister a confused look. "That's nice, but I thought you were going to look for a little dog—"

"No. I don't want a little dog. Harley's the best dog here. He's going to Mr. Woodson's house, but I can still go see him and be friends with him there. Right, Mom?"

"We'll talk about it." Savannah spoke briskly. "But now it's time for us to leave and for Harley to get his supper."

"I'm going to take him in right now," Drew said.

"Can I go with him, Mom?" Gracie pleaded. "So I can say goodbye to Harley? Please?"

Savannah's eyes clouded with uncertainty. "I don't—"

Gracie and Drew spoke at the same time:

"I won't cry or anything, I promise."

"We won't be gone long."

Savannah gave in. "All right." She gave her daughter a steady look. "But I'm counting on you to keep your promise."

Gracie nodded eagerly. "I will."

As she and Drew took the dog back to the main building, she asked "Can I tell you a secret?"

A flutter of unease moved through him. What was this

about? "I don't think we should keep secrets from your mom."

"Oh, it's not a *bad* secret," Gracie answered quickly. "I know you're not supposed to keep those. It's about Harley."

"Uh-huh?"

"If Harley goes to live with you, I can visit him, right? And help teach him to be good. You said I could, remember?"

"Of course." And he'd meant it. Remembering Savannah's accusations, he again felt their sharp sting. He didn't lie to kids.

"Well, if we can teach him and show Mom what a good dog he is, then she'll change her mind about him. She'll let him come live with us. Isn't that a good plan?"

Drew admired how her little mind worked. One the one hand, it wasn't a bad plan. On the other hand, he didn't want to give her false hope. "Didn't your mom say something about your landlord? What's his name?"

Gracie's forehead crumpled. "Mr. Russo." She thought for a moment, then brightened. "We can tell him that Harley will be a good protector. He'll keep burglars away."

We? Gracie apparently considered him her co-conspirator in this plot to win over her mother and Mr. Russo.

Well, why not? He'd not only be helping Gracie. He'd be seeing that Harley found a forever home. After all, a foster placement was only temporary. He couldn't keep the dog indefinitely even if he wanted to. His life was too complicated and about to get more so.

"Mr. Woodson?" Gracie gazed up at him, her eyes big. "Will you help me?"

How could he refuse? "I'll help you, Gracie. But please don't be too disappointed if it doesn't work out. Sometimes things don't work out the way we hope, no matter how hard we try."

That possibility didn't seem to enter her mind. She gave him a big smile. "It *will* work. You'll see."

Inside the building, they went to the front desk. Walter stood there, along with a woman.

"Hi," Drew said. "I'm just returning Harley." He tried not to look at the dog, who gave a soft whimper. *"Please don't send me back,"* his pleading eyes seemed to say.

Gracie curled her arms around Harley's neck and kissed the top of his head. "Don't be sad," she told him. "It's just for a little while."

"I'll take him back," Walter said, gently extricating him from Gracie's embrace. "Let's go, Harl. It's supper time. Did you have a fun day?"

The dog gave a sharp woof, making them all laugh.

"That's a yes," Walter said. "Come on, guy."

Harley whimpered again and cast a longing glance at Gracie.

"Bye-bye, Harley," she said. "See you soon."

As Harley was led away, Savannah entered the building. "Gracie? Are you ready?"

"Yes, Mom."

Savannah gave Drew a quick look. "Don't forget to thank Mr. Woodson for letting us spend the day with him and Harley." She spoke stiffly, as though it were an effort to remember her manners.

Gracie responded obediently. "Thank you, Mr. Woodson." Then, turning so only he could see her, she wiggled her eyebrows and gave him a secret smile. A smile that said *"Don't forget our plan."*

I won't, he promised silently. When she and her mother left, he spoke to the woman behind the desk. "I'd like to find out more about fostering a pet."

CHAPTER 7

Harley

I live with the man named Drew now. He is nice to me and I like him very much. I miss Walter and some of the other dogs from Happy Hearts, but I do not miss my cage at all.

Now I am never in a cage. I live with Drew in a big house near the lake. I like the lake! It is cool and wet and feels so good on a hot day. At my old house, my cat friend and I would play Chase then we would jump in the lake and swim. It was fun. I wish the man and I could go swimming but when I try to go down there, he just says "No, no."

He is teaching me, and it is a little bit fun. Not as fun as swimming but I get a treat when I do something Good and I like treats. They taste yummy.

I am learning things like Sit and Stay. We practice a lot and now when I hear Sit my bottom goes down right away and the man tells me "Good." I am so happy when he says that, I want to jump and bounce but that would be Bad. So I sit still, even though it is hard, until the man says "Come."

I love to Come to Drew. It is easy because he is my friend.

Stay is very hard because I do not like to stay away from my friend. I like to be near him. I must wait and wait until my whole body itches and feels like I can't be still one second longer. I whimper a bit because I want to wiggle and wriggle but I try to be Good.

"Good" is the best word in the world. It feels to my ears like a big juicy steak feels to my tummy. It makes my tail wag and makes me warm and happy inside.

I want to be a Good Dog and make my friend proud. Then he will love me and keep me forever.

Sometimes it is quiet and a little lonely with just us two, so we play games to have fun. I made up a game called Chase Me. I take a dish towel from the refrigerator door and prance around with it in my mouth. Then he chases me and tries to catch me to put the towel back where it belongs. I run around the chairs and under the table. We have so much fun because I am fast and hard to catch! It is a good game.

Today Drew hid the dish towel, so I have come up with another fun game called This is Smelly. There is a big can in the kitchen that my friend puts things in. Things like carrot ends and potato peels and shriveled up pieces of baloney. I don't know why he puts them there when I would like to eat them. I guess he likes them too because he saves them in the can until they turn very smelly.

I love smelly things. They make my nose very, very happy. So today I will make my friend happy too. I stick my head in the big can and take something out to share with him. It is brown and slimy and smells very interesting.

Oops! By mistake I knock the big can over and more smelly things spill out onto the floor. It is all right, though, because I pick the best one for my friend. I am proud to share it with him. It is good to share.

I carry it into the room where he sits in the big chair and drop it on his lap. But my friend doesn't like it. He frowns and jumps up and lets it fall to the floor. "Ugh! No, Harley! That's disgusting."

Disgusting? What does that mean?

He hurries away and I hear him say some bad words when he finds the big can tipped over in the kitchen. Things go clunk and splat as he cleans up. I am alone with the smelly thing. I nudge it with my nose...I sniff and snuffle it...

Drew comes back with a handful of paper towels. He frowns angrily, wiping the slimy stuff from his pants.

"I can't believe you knocked over the garbage," he grumbles. "That was bad."

I whimper sadly. I did not mean to be Bad.

He stops and looks around the floor. "Where did it go?"

Uh-oh. My tummy rumbles and a big burp comes out of me.

"Harley!" he cries. "Did you eat it? That's gross!"

Gross must be Bad, like disgusting. My head droops in shame. I did not know it was gross to eat the smelly thing. It tasted fine to me.

Then his forehead crinkles. "My gosh, I hope you don't get sick." He frowns again, but this time he doesn't look angry. He looks worried. "I better call the vet."

He goes into the bedroom for a while I lie on the living room floor. My tummy feels rumbly and I am confused. Why is it Bad to be gross and disgusting? Why doesn't my friend like the nice things I like?

If the things I like are Bad, what does it mean to be Good?

I am very confused.

He comes back in a little while, his face relieved. "Well, the vet said it probably wouldn't make you sick. But just to be on the safe side, think I'll put you outdoors for a few."

I look up at him and whine. I do not like to be In the Yard by myself. My other family put me In the Yard when I was

Bad. It was lonesome all by myself. I do not like to be lonesome. I want to be with my friend Drew.

He puts me In the Yard anyway. But I am not too sad because he rubs my head and gives me a funny crooked smile. "It's my fault, too, bud. I know you were just doing your thing. I've got to do a better job of dog-proofing the place."

My tail wags. I am glad he is not mad at me. He still likes me.

When he goes inside, I sigh and lie down on the grass. I try to think more about the secret of being Good. Birds chirp in the trees, bees buzz in the flowers and the breeze makes the red and yellow leaves rustle over my head. I close my eyes and drift away...

Then I hear a voice. "Hey, wake up! What, you're sleeping, you big goof?"

My head pops up. Who said that? It was not my friend Drew.

A bush near the fence rustles and an orange cat wriggles out. "Hiya, Fuzz for Brains! Long time no see."

I jump to my feet oh so happy happy! It is my cat friend named Boots! He was my neighbor at my other house and when I used to visit him we would play and have lots of fun. We were good friends and he called me names like Fuzzhead and Goofball because he liked me so much.

I like him, too. I race over to him and give him a big lick to say Hi. His fur tastes funny on my tongue but he smells good like fishy cat food and kitty litter.

"Yah," he cries, falling over. "Watch out. You're slobbering all over me, guy."

I back up a little to let him stand up again, but it is so hard to be still. My heart is a balloon that wants to float up to the sky. My tail goes round and round.

"Hey, I brung a friend," Boots says. The bush rustles again

and a very fluffy gray cat pokes out his head. It is my other cat friend named Zeno!

"What you waiting for?" Boots asks him. "Come on out."

"Umph. I'm trying. I think my fur is tangled in the twigs."

"Maybe you're a little too chubby," Boots says. "You been putting on weight, you know. You almost got stuck under that fence we snuck under."

"I most certainly did not, and I'll thank you not to comment on my weight." Zeno's voice is grumbly. "I'm just the right size for a cat of my build."

"Okay, okay. Want me to give you a little nudge or something?"

"No, I do not want a…umph." He tugs hard and steps out of the bush. Some little leaves are stuck in his fur. "There. I'm free. Hello, Harley."

My two good friends remembered me! They came all this way to see me! I want to sniff them and lick them a million times. So much happiness fills me that I can't keep still. I must yip and prance and race round and round to show my friends how much I like them—

"Harley, for goodness' sake, sit still."

When Zeno says the magic word *Sit* my bottom plops down on the ground. I am a little bit surprised that my bottom knows what to do before my head does but I am glad, too. It means my bottom is smart because Drew and I practice Sit all the time.

"Wow, look at that," Boots says, his green eyes wide. "He did just what you said, Zeno. That was good, Fuzzhead."

Good fills my chest all warm and happy. I smile and my tail goes wag wag.

And there's something else. I can understand what they are saying! At my old house, I could only understand a little bit of cat talk. Most of what my friends said sounded like "Meow, meow, rowl, mewl, hiss."

But now their sounds are words and I understand them! It means my head is getting smarter, along with my bottom. I give a big woof to show my friends I know what they said.

"We wondered what happened when you just disappeared from the neighborhood," Boots says. "One day you were in your yard as usual and the next day, poof, you were gone."

"Yes, and we were worried," Zeno says. "We didn't know what to think."

I whimper softly. My friends cared about me. I am sad to know they worried.

"Then we heard about the crummy trick your people played, giving you away." Boots' eyes become slits and his voice turns to a growl. "Man, that was a rotten thing to do."

"It certainly was." Zeno slashes his fluffy tail. "You were never a bad dog, just high spirited. They should have been more patient with you."

"Yeah, and let me tell you," Boots adds. "Those people better stay on their side of the fence from now on, cause if they come into *my* yard? Watch out, brother."

"*I* don't even acknowledge them," Zeno says. "If I see them, I simply hiss and turn my back."

"But see, Zeno's guy Ty is buds with your guy. That's how we found out you're here. So we came over to like check up on you. See if you're doing okay." Boots glances around the yard. "Looks like a pretty sweet deal you got going here. Still on the lake and close enough for us to come over sometimes. What about your guy, what's his name?"

"Drew," Zeno answers.

"Yeah, this Drew. He treat you okay?"

I woof yes. Drew is my friend, and he is very nice to me.

"Good. Glad to hear it. Cause if he don't, him and me are gonna have a problem."

"Oh, for goodness' sake, Boots. Drew is a fine person." Zeno is talking now. "He's been a very good friend to Tyson.

And he'll be good to you too, Harley. This is a fresh start for you. I'm telling you this because I'm your friend: it's time you stop acting like a silly pup. You need to grow up and behave like a good dog."

Yes. My friend Zeno is right. I want to be a Good Dog more than anything in the whole world.

If only I can find out the secret to being Good…

CHAPTER 8

Drew

"Wait. Hold on a minute," Adrienne said as they spoke via video chat. "You did what, now?"

His sister arched one eyebrow and pursed her lips, giving him *that look*—the one that asked, *"What in heaven's name is going on in that head of yours?"*

He'd seen that skeptical expression before—the one that made her look like a disapproving schoolteacher. All she needed was a pair of spectacles perched on the end of her nose to complete the picture. It had been funny when she was a little kid, shaking her head over her big brother's knuckleheaded antics. Now that they were both adults, it wasn't quite so funny.

"You heard me right," he answered. "I'm fostering a dog."

"A dog," she repeated. "What brought this about?"

"Oh, it was…a spur of the moment thing, I guess you'd say." He wasn't ready to tell her about Gracie and Savannah yet.

"I guess so," she murmured, her dark curls swaying as she

shook her head. Apparently, she'd given up any hope of understanding him. "Okay, dogfather, is there any chance of getting a look at him? Or is it her?"

"He's a male. Wait, he's right here." Drew flipped out of selfie mode and focused the camera on the dog, who was lying on the rug nearby. "Come here, Harley. Come say hi to my sister." Technically his stepsister, but he and Adrienne never fussed over that detail.

Harley's ears perked up and he trotted over to Drew, then stuck his nose up to the phone.

Adrienne laughed. "He's a big boy, isn't he? Well, I have to admit he's cute."

"He's cute, yeah." Drew yanked the phone away when Harley tried to lick the screen. "And full of it. Okay, that's enough," he told the dog. "Go lie down now. Good boy."

Harley gave a happy huff and planted his butt on the floor beside Drew's chair.

"Is he lying down?" Adrienne asked when Drew flipped the screen back again.

He gave the dog a rueful side-eye. "Uh, no. We haven't mastered all the commands yet. He's good at 'Sit,' though."

Harley woofed as though saying *"Yes!"*

"How are the girls doing?" Drew asked. Adrienne and her husband had adopted a pair of Corgis a year or so back.

"Just fine. I'd show you, but they're in the bedroom snoozing."

"On the bed?"

Adrienne chuckled. "Oh, they'd love that. But their short little legs can't get them up that high." Then the smile faded from her pretty, brown face. "You certainly have become mysterious lately."

The sudden turnabout in conversation surprised him. "How's that?"

"Well, first you up and quit your show—"

"I didn't quit," he replied, shifting uncomfortably in his seat. "I'm just, uh, taking a break. That's all." As Executive Producer and host of the sports talk show, he could have placed it on hiatus. That would have meant putting the crew and other employees out of work, which he didn't want. The network had scrambled to find a replacement host, but otherwise *All in the Game* was doing just fine.

"It came clear out of the blue, though. Mom and Pop said you never talked it over with them. And you certainly never mentioned it to me."

Irritation needled him. "I didn't realize I had to clear my business decisions with my family first."

"Nobody's saying that. But you could have at least given the folks a head's up instead of letting them find out about it online."

He suppressed a groan. Yeah, that hadn't worked out well. He'd gotten a worried phone call from Mom, who was afraid something terrible had happened to him. He'd also received an angry text from Pop, reaming him out for upsetting his mother. *What's wrong with you, boy?*

"I know. My bad," he answered. "But I had to move fast."

Alarm sharpened his sister's features. "What's that mean?"

Oh, crap. He hadn't meant to let that slip. "Uh, it's just…it was getting to me," he said, quickly backtracking. "The pressure, I mean. I was getting burned out big time. I had to take a break." Which wasn't true. While he'd enjoyed the show, he'd been feeling restless, though he couldn't put his finger on the source of his dissatisfaction. He might have drifted along that way indefinitely—if not for the unwelcome reappearance of someone he'd long ago forgotten.

But he had no intention of telling Adrienne or anyone in his family his real reasons for stepping down. He had to protect them.

Time for a change of topic. "Enough about me. What's going on in your life? How's Jordan?"

His sister's mouth flattened. "Oh. He's well. As far as I know. I barely see him anymore."

Her shuttered expression and clipped response alarmed Drew. He sat up in his chair so abruptly that Harley yipped in surprise. "What's going on, sis?"

"I don't know. He's never home. And when he is, we don't talk. Not about anything important."

Stunned, Drew didn't know what to say. Adrienne and Jordan connected in college and had been in love ever since. They married right after graduation, and since then had focused on their careers. Though Drew had been tough on some of his baby sister's former boyfriends, he'd always liked Jordan. He was a genuinely good guy and one of the few men worthy of Adrienne.

A nasty suspicion crept into his mind. "Do you think he's...?" He didn't want to utter the word *cheating*. He wouldn't have suspected it of Jordan, but if the man was never home...

She let go a hopeless sigh. "I don't know what's going on. He says it's work. But I can't get more out of him that that. He won't discuss anything with me. Just pushes me away."

"What about counseling or something?"

She gave a sad little laugh. "If he won't talk to me, do you really think he's going to sit down with a counselor? If I could even get him there."

"I'm sorry, sis. Whatever happens, I'm here for you always. You know that, right?"

Her lips quirked in a smile, but her eyes remained sad. "Of course, I do. Look, don't worry. I guess these things just happen."

What things? Drew wondered. But Adrienne wasn't

saying. Looked like he wasn't the only one in the family with a secret.

"You know you can call me anytime."

"I know. I love you, bruh."

"Love you back. Take care."

"You, too. Bye." With that, she ended the call.

Drew sat there, still stunned by his sister's news. Sure, married couples had their ups and downs, but Adrienne and Jordan always seemed so happy together. Drew knew how much his sister loved her husband and he'd have sworn Jordan was just as devoted.

Adrienne wasn't a woman who gave up easily on the people she loved. She fought tooth and nail for them. Now all the fight seemed to have drained out of her. Only something big would do that to her.

Something huge.

Harley came up to him and nudged his arm, a confused look on his face. *What's the matter?*

Drew patted the dog's head. "Hey, you."

Harley gave a happy huff, nudging him again. *Keep going.*

"Yeah, you'd let me do that all day, wouldn't you?" Drew grinned. One thing about this dog—he was a sure cure for a bad mood. He was so jolly and silly, his good humor was contagious.

"Hey, what time is it?" Drew glanced at his watch. "Come on, guy. We've got somewhere to be."

Harley followed him to the door, prancing impatiently while Drew attached his leash. "Yeah. Good boy. We're going to meet your friends. Gracie and her mom. Remember them?"

The dog barked and his tail waved like a flag.

"I'll take that as a yes."

He only hoped Gracie and Savannah would be at the park when he and Harley arrived. Ty and his girl Shelley would be there, and Shelley had promised she'd try to get her sister and niece to come, too. He hoped she'd be successful. Then he'd know he'd done his part to keep his bargain with Gracie.

"But first, we've got a stop to make."

* * *

The Lakeside Court Motel wasn't the fanciest place to stay in Verona Lake, but it was by no means the shabbiest, either. Frank hadn't complained when Drew got him a room there. "It's nicer than most of the places I've flopped," Frank had said. "Trust me."

Trust him? No, Drew wasn't prepared to do that. Not at all.

It wasn't the cost that concerned him. Lakeside Court was a bit more secluded than some of the other spots in town. There were fewer people to notice and wonder about someone's coming and going. Fewer people to ask nosy questions and get in one's business.

Which made it easier to keep a low profile.

The motel housed single rooms that faced a parking lot. Though Drew didn't plan on staying long, he didn't want to leave the rambunctious dog alone in the car to chew the upholstery or get into some other mischief. Once he parked the car, he attached Harley's leash to his collar and led him to Room 26.

There was no answer when he knocked at the door.

He frowned. Where could Frank be? Maybe he'd gone out to one of the nearby restaurants or diners within walking distance, though it was well past lunch time. Maybe he was just out for a stroll, getting some fresh air.

Yeah, right. Fresh air. The guy who reeks of cigarettes, who can't walk more than a few feet without wheezing.

He knocked again, harder. "Frank. Hey. You in there?" He

could hear the TV playing in the room. Some true crime show. A sense of unease crept through him. Why wasn't the man answering?

Drew wanted to kick himself for even caring. *What's it to you? You're not this guy's keeper. It's not like he ever gave a care about you all these years. He probably just up and skipped town. With no goodbye. Without a word. That's his style, right?*

The uneasy feeling turned to cold dread. What if Frank hadn't skipped? What if he *couldn't* answer the door? He was in terrible health and those stupid cigarettes didn't help matters. What if he was sick? What if he'd had a heart attack or passed out from a stroke?

If he's passed out, it's from too many beers. Forget about him. You don't owe him anything. You've already done more for him than he's ever done for you.

He ought to just get back in the car and take off. Let Frank worry about himself. That's what anyone with a lick of sense would do.

But because he had no sense, he decided to go to the main office and ask them to check the room. He'd never be able to live with himself otherwise.

He glanced down at Harley. "Okay, dude. They won't let you in the office, so it's back in the car for you while I try to solve this mystery."

He had just gotten to the car when a voice called "Hey! You looking for me?"

Frank Flanagan sat in a lawn chair by the outdoor pool, waving him over.

Drew stiffened as relief washed through him, quickly followed by irritation. He gave Harley's leash a gentle tug. "Come on, boy."

He took the empty seat beside Frank. They were the only ones out by the pool, which had been drained and covered over at the end of summer. Harley, his tongue lolling and tail wagging, pranced eagerly up to Frank.

Frank grinned and scrubbed the dog's head with his knuckles. "Hey, who's this guy?"

"His name's Harley. I'm uh, fostering him for a while."

"Yeah?" Frank gave Harley another scrub between the ears. The dog woofed happily.

"Harley, sit." Drew spoke sharply, irked at how easily the dog accepted Frank. Weren't animals supposed to be good judges of character?

Harley swiftly obeyed the command. Drew's annoyance disappeared and he forgave Harley instantly. "Good boy." *Don't blame him. He's just a big knucklehead. He wants everybody to like him.*

Frank glanced from the dog to Drew. "Nice looking dog. Makes me think of Boomer. Remember him?"

"Of course, I do," Drew snapped, ticked off again. *Not likely I'd forget him. He was the only thing that got me through after you bailed on Mom and me. He was more loyal than you ever were.*

Frank looked away. "Didn't expect you today. Thought you'd let me know when you planned to stop by."

Right. Like the way you let me know when you skipped town all those years ago.

"I knocked on your door. Heard the TV going. When you didn't answer, I—"

"What? Thought I'd dropped dead or something?" Frank gave a huff of laughter than turned into a smoker's hack. His hunched shoulders shook. When he finally stopped coughing, he wiped wetness from his eyes. "Or maybe you were hoping."

Drew let that one pass. "Just wondered if there's anything you need."

"Need? Nah, I'm all set. Got plenty left from what you gave me the other day. I don't need much. I go to the diner on the corner for my meals. Getting to be a regular there. Got my smokes—" he patted his shirt pocket. "What else would I need?"

As if on cue, he pulled a cigarette from the pack and lit up. His bony hands shook as he struck the match.

Drew's mouth flattened. *Keep puffing on those things, they'll fix you right up.* "Isn't this supposed to be a smoke-free zone?"

Frank shrugged, then looked around. "Who's gonna complain?"

Drew clamped his lips shut, swallowing his anger. *Let it go. The guy's a wreck. A few more cigarettes aren't going to make any difference.*

Anyone looking at Frank could see the toll years of hard living had taken. He was as stringy as a piece of jerky. His skin was a yellowish-gray, his eyes rheumy, his stubbled cheeks sunken. His fingertips were tinged yellow by the nicotine of thousands of cigarettes. Every time Drew looked at him, he felt a wave of pity and revulsion.

Why's he here, after all this time? What's he want from me?

He had yet to figure that out.

"I got tired of sitting inside," Frank said, as though he were answering a question. "Thought I'd come out here for a while. I watch the cars go by. It's nice and peaceful. At my age, that's the best you can hope for. A little peace."

Was that really all he wanted?

As though he read Drew's mind, Frank added "And a chance to know my son."

The word *son* scraped Drew's nerves like a grater. *You lost the right to call me son long ago. When you threw me and Mom away and left us like trash on the side of the road.*

He jerked to his feet, inadvertently yanking Harley's collar, causing him to yip. He stroked the dog's head in apology. "Sorry, dude." To Frank, he said "I'm going to take off now. I'm meeting some friends."

"Oh." A disappointed look passed over the older man's face, but quickly disappeared. "Sure. The dog's going, too?"

"Yes."

"All right." He scratched Harley's ears. "Well, you have fun, boy."

The dog smiled and huffed in joy. Drew wrapped the leash around one hand and dug into his pocket with the other. He pulled several bills from his wallet. "Here. Take this, just in case."

Frank shook his head. "I told you, I'm fine."

"Take it." He thrust them at Frank, angry at the man, but angrier at himself. *He drops back into my life like nothing ever happened and I'm the one who feels guilty.*

Just because he couldn't open his arms and say, "All is forgiven." Because he wasn't ready to hug it out and be best buds with the old man.

Because he was waiting for the other shoe to drop.

Frank took the cash reluctantly, folding the bills into his front pocket. "Okay. Well, maybe next time you can stay a little longer."

"Maybe." Drew's voice was stiff. His body felt wooden. "Next time." He gave Harley's leash a gentle tug. "Come on, boy."

He got the dog into the back seat and took his own place behind the wheel, suddenly exhausted. He had to snap out of it, though. Be at his best when he met Gracie and her mom at the park.

He'd picked one heck of a time to get involved with a little girl and a goofy dog while trying to handle this whole mess with Frank. *Way to complicate your life, dude. As if it wasn't complicated enough.*

Frank was the reason he'd stepped down from his talk

show. The reason he was lying low here in Verona Lake. Anyone would be shaken up to have their deadbeat dad reappear after decades of radio silence. When that *anyone* was a former Major League player and a current television personality, it was more than life-shaking. It was newsworthy.

Drew knew the deal. He was used to his name showing up online, in newspapers, blogs, and gossip columns going back years. He might not always love it, but as public figure he'd signed up for it.

His family hadn't.

His mother didn't deserve to have her life upended by the reappearance of the husband who'd abandoned her years ago. Neither did Pop, his stepfather, who'd been more of a dad than Frank had ever been. His sister Adrienne, worrying over the state of her marriage, shouldn't have to deal with smarmy gossip.

He had to protect them until he could suss out Frank's real reason for suddenly dropping into his life.

Why now? Why, after all these years?

That was his first question when Frank started sending him private messages. Drew had ignored the first few. He was used to the occasional rando reaching out, usually with some scam. But he began taking the messages seriously when Frank shared information that only Drew's donor—Drew refused to call him *father*—would know.

Ultimately curiosity got the best of him, and Drew agreed to a meeting. Or maybe it had been more than curiosity. Drew wanted to stare the man down, rub his nose in his success: *"Look at me. You see this suit? It's custom made. These shoes? They're Italian. Hand sewn. The car I drive costs more than your house. I've got friends, a family that loves me, and more money than you'll see in a lifetime. Ten lifetimes. None of it thanks to you. You walked out on me like I was nothing. Well, I'm not nothing anymore, friend. How d'you like me now?"*

But shocked by how run down and ragged Frank looked, he'd said none of that. Instead, at their first meeting Drew had blurted "So, what? Are you dying or something? Got like six months to live and looking to clear your conscience? Grab some cheap forgiveness before you kick off?"

Frank had laughed at the proposition. "Nah. Nothing like that. Sounds like something out of a movie."

It did at that. A movie too sappy to sit through. In spite of himself, Drew had cracked a smile.

"You looking for money, then? And if I don't come across, you'll go to some rag and spill your guts? 'Former Athlete Lives Large While His Father Lives in Poverty.' That'd make a juicy story."

Frank had looked thoughtful. "Huh. Hadn't thought of that. Thanks for the tip, though."

A huff of laughter escaped Drew, which he immediately turned into a cough. Under different circumstances, he could almost like this guy.

Don't forget what he did. Don't let him forget, either.

"Look, if you want a few bucks, whatever, tell me straight out. Don't try to play me. I've got no time for that."

"That's what I want."

Drew blinked. Okay, that was right to the point. Still, it stung to hear. He wanted to kick himself. *What's wrong with you, stupid? Of course, it's about money. Why else would he be here?*

"All right." Drew made sure his voice betrayed no emotion. "How much, then?" Whatever the amount, it would be worth it to make sure this guy got lost and stayed lost.

Frank shook his head. "Not your money. Your time. That's what I want from you. I know I got no right to ask, but I'd like to spend some time with you. Get to know my son."

My son. The words crawled up Drew's spine like a

centipede, making him hunch his shoulders defensively. "You lost the right to ever call me that. And if you don't know me, it's your doing."

"Yeah. It's on me, I get that. Just the same…" Frank pinned him with a stare. "What do you say?"

Drew's first impulse was to laugh in his face. *I don't owe you a thing.*

But he held himself in check. He didn't know why Frank suddenly wanted to get close after years of silence. Drew didn't trust him. The old man had made a joke of going to the tabloids, but who could say that wasn't on his agenda? Drew didn't care what kind of slop the rags might throw his way, but he didn't want his family dirtied by their muck. His mom, his stepdad, Adrienne…they deserved better.

He had to protect them.

An old adage popped into his head: *Keep your friends close and your enemies closer.* Frank was no friend, and he had the potential to become an enemy.

Better to tease this out than spit in the guy's face. Find out what this was really all about.

And best to do it somewhere private, out of the public eye. In a small town like Verona Lake. Drew would keep Frank tucked away at Lakeside Court for a while. And if he were stringing the old man along, keeping him at a distance and stopping by only when it suited him, so what? Hadn't Frank strung Drew along for years, making him wait and wonder if his father would ever come home?

Now Frank could learn what it felt like. Waiting and wondering.

And if Drew felt guilty about it from time to time, it only went to show what a soft-hearted jerk he was.

Get over it, he told himself. *Frank's lucky you give him the time of day. He's staying at a nice place, all expenses paid, on your dime. He's got no beef.*

From the car's back seat, Harley gave a small woof, as though asking *"What are we waiting for?"*

That knocked Drew back to the present. He gave a short laugh and turned on the car's ignition. "Okay, buddy. We're on our way."

He'd get over it, all right. And have it together by the time he and Harley reached the park.

For Gracie's sake.

CHAPTER 9

Savannah

It was only after Savannah and Gracie arrived to join Shelley and her boyfriend Ty for a picnic in the park that Shelley dropped the other shoe: "Oh, by the way, Drew will be joining us."

Gracie's eyes lit up. "He will?"

Shelley grinned. "Yes, and he said he'd bring Harley."

"Oh boy, oh boy!" Gracie hopped with excitement. "Did you hear, Mom? Harley's coming!"

"Yes, I heard." Savannah struggled to keep her smile in place while sending her sister an evil look. "Go see if Ty needs any help getting stuff from the car."

When Gracie skipped away, Savannah muttered "Thanks a lot."

Giving her the innocent act, Shelley shrugged. "What's the problem, sis?"

"The problem is, I've been trying to wean Gracie off thinking about Harley." Not that she'd had much luck. They'd made another trip to Happy Hearts to look at more dogs, but while Gracie eyed them compassionately, she wanted none of them. "No, Mom. They're nice, but…"

Though her voice trailed off, Savannah knew what Gracie left unspoken: *"They're not Harley."*

When Savannah suggested another visit, hoping time would lessen her daughter's devotion to the Black Lab, Gracie shook her head. "No. It makes me sad to go there and see all the dogs with no families. I wish we could take them all home."

So do I, Savannah thought. And though she was touched by her daughter's tender heart, she was more than frustrated with Gracie's stubbornness.

"Nothing I've tried seems to make a dent," she told Shelley. "When she gets her mind made up about something, that's it."

Shelley gave a short laugh. "Gee, I wonder where she gets that from."

Savannah shot her a dirty look. "Oh, be quiet."

"Come on, what's the harm?" Shelley went on. "It'll give Gracie a chance to see Harley again. Didn't you see how happy she was? And you can—"

"I can what?" Annoyance made Savannah's voice sharp. She didn't appreciate feeling ambushed.

"You can get to know Drew a little better."

"And why would I want to do that?"

"Cause he's a nice guy. And how long has it been you've—"

"Hold on." Savannah jerked up her hand to stop any further discussion. "Please tell me you're not doing any matchmaking here."

Shelley looked away guiltily. "Well, no, but—"

"No buts. I am not in the market for a man. And if I were, I certainly wouldn't want my kid sister scrounging up dates for me. Like I can't get anybody on my own."

"You're not even trying. Drew Woodson is successful, handsome, rich—not to mention hot as blazes. If that's *scrounging*, then I don't know what—"

"He might be all that and a bag of chips, but I'm not looking. I've got everything I need."

Shelley locked eyes with her. "A wall is what you've got. A wall with a big fat sign on it that says 'No Entrance.' And you won't let anyone through. You say Gracie's stubborn? Because one man did you wrong, you decided that all men are lying cheats and you'll never trust another one. Tell me how that's fair. How it makes any sense."

Red hot rage shot through Savannah. Shelley knew what she'd been through. How Gracie's father had abandoned her and his unborn child. How could her own sister throw the past in her face? How could Shelley mock her for wanting to protect herself and her little girl?

She'd been hurt once but it hadn't destroyed her. Gracie had given her a reason to keep struggling and succeed. She was in a good place now. She and Gracie were safe. If she wasn't ready to risk her heart again, that was her business. Not her sister's. Not anyone's.

"I'm not discussing this with you. If we can't drop it, then I'm just going to get Gracie and take her home."

"Wait." Shelley's expression softened and she touched Savannah's arm. "Don't go. I didn't mean to upset you. Please don't disappoint Gracie. She's really looking forward to this. I'm sorry. Forget what I said about...you know."

"All right." She'd try to forget, but it wouldn't be easy. Especially since a tiny part of her knew that everything Shelley had said about walls was true. "But no trying to push us together. Understood?"

Shelley nodded meekly. "Drew's a nice guy. He's been a real good friend to Ty. And to me. Nothing wrong with making another friend, is there?"

"No. I suppose not." But she couldn't lie to herself. Drew Woodson was everything Shelley had described—handsome, hot, successful. Savannah could be very attracted to him, if she let herself.

That's the rub. And there's only one solution. Don't let yourself.

"They're here!" Gracie cried. Savannah turned to watch her daughter run to greet Harley, who tugged at the leash in Drew Woodson's hand. He yipped and pranced in excitement.

"Harley!" Gracie flung her arms around the dog's neck. "I missed you."

The dog sat, accepting her hug with a big doggy grin, and swiped her cheek with his tongue.

Gracie drew back, laughing. "He kissed me!"

"Don't you say hello to Mr. Woodson?" Her mother asked. "Harley wouldn't be here without him."

"Hi, Mr. Woodson." Though Gracie spoke politely, she barely spared him a glance. Harley had her full attention.

Savannah gave him an apologetic smile, but Drew seemed to take no offense. He greeted Ty and Shelley and gave Savannah a friendly hello. Then he smiled down at Gracie and Harley. "Don't get him too excited, now. I don't want him to forget everything he's learned."

Gracie's eyebrows lifted. "Does he know some tricks?"

"We're still working on some basic commands. But he's doing well. He's a smart guy. Aren't you, boy?"

Harley huffed as though he agreed.

Drew's smile faded when he glanced at the picnic table set with paper plates, cups, and utensils. "Are we eating? I wish I'd known. I'd have brought something."

"Don't sweat it," Ty said as he unloaded some deli sandwiches from a bag. "We figured as long as we're getting together, might as well make an early dinner out of it."

"That's okay," Gracie said. "You brought Harley. That's the main thing."

Drew asked "Can I help with anything?"

Ty eyed the dog, who gazed longingly at the sandwiches. "For now, just keep our friend there away from the food."

"Okay. Come on, Harley. You already ate."

"Show us his tricks!" Gracie cried excitedly.

"Okay. Let's move over here." He led the dog away from the table to a patch of grass under a tree. Gracie followed.

Drew took something from his pocket and stood to face the dog, whose eyes were riveted to him. "Harley. Sit."

Harley obeyed and was rewarded with a treat.

Gracie clapped. "Yay, Harley!" Then, to Drew: "What did you give him?"

"It's a kind of cookie he likes. I break it into little pieces and give him one when he sits."

"I like cookies." Gracie eyed him hopefully.

"Do you like chicken flavored cookies? That's his favorite."

Her mouth twisted in disgust. "Chicken cookies? Yuck."

Drew laughed. "They're made specially for dogs, hon. Not for people." Then he said "Hey. Would you like him to sit for you?"

"Could I?"

"Sure. I'll show you. Here." He had her move beside him to face Harley, then gave her a piece of cookie. "Take this. Curl your hand around it like a fist. That's good. Then just raise your arm so it's over his head and he has to look up at you." Drew guided her to slowly follow his instructions. "See, he knows the treat's in your hand. When he looks up, he has to lower his butt to the ground. Now tell him 'sit.'"

"Sit, Harley."

The dog obeyed, planting his hind end as he stared up at Gracie's closed fist.

"Now tell him he's a good boy and let him have the treat."

"Good boy, Harley." She opened her fist and Harley caught the treat as it fell. "He did it!"

"Yeah. You did a great job, Gracie."

Gracie beamed. "Thanks."

Taking in the scene, Savannah found herself smiling. A melting warmth suffused her as she saw how happy and proud her daughter was. Drew dealt with Gracie as easily as he did with Harley.

"Van. Van." Shelley nudged her.

"Huh?" She blinked, suddenly aware of her sister's presence.

"I asked if you wanted water to drink or iced tea." She held a bottle in each hand.

Savannah flushed, embarrassed at being caught unaware. "Oh. Um, water's fine. Thanks."

Shelley nodded toward Drew and Gracie. "He's good with her, isn't he?"

"Yes, he…" Savannah gave her sister a suspicious look. Was she still playing matchmaker?

Shelley expression was bland and innocent. "Water it is."

"Food's on," Ty called, setting down a bag of chips. "Come and get it, everyone."

"I want to sit next to Harley!" Gracie called as she raced over. Harley gave a happy woof.

"He can't be at the table," Drew told her. "But if you sit here at this end, he can lie on the grass near you." He tied the dog's leash to a leg of the picnic bench. "That should hold him while we eat."

With Shelley and Ty together on one side of the table, and Gracie on the other side, Savannah found herself shoulder to shoulder with Drew. There didn't seem to be any polite way to avoid sitting next to him. She returned Shelley's little smirk with a narrow look—it was a setup, all right—but made up her mind not to let her annoyance show. She'd take the high road, rise above Shelley's little scheme, and not give her sister the satisfaction of a reaction.

Turning to Drew, she politely asked if he'd care for some potato salad. Then she noticed Gracie trying to offer the dog a corn chip. "Gracie, no. Don't do that."

"Your mom's right, hon," Drew added. "That chip's not good for him. Besides, he already ate something today he shouldn't have."

"What did he do?" Gracie crunched the chip herself while Harley whimpered in disappointment.

"He managed to get into the garbage can and drag something out. I guess he wanted to share it with me, cause he plopped it right in my lap. I went to get some paper towels to clean up and when I came back..." he shrugged. "It was gone."

"He ate it?" Gracie's eyes were round. "Harley, yuck."

Harley grinned and wagged his tail, as though he'd done something to be proud of.

"How did he get in the garbage can?"

"It's one of those things where you step on a pedal and the lid opens. He's probably seen me do it so often that he figured it out. He stepped on the thing, opened the lid, and helped himself." Drew shook his head. "I'm going to have to do a better job of dog proofing my place."

"He's smart, if he knew how to do it just from watching," Gracie said.

"Yeah, he is. We just have to make sure he learns the right things and not the naughty ones."

"That's right." Gracie nodded emphatically in agreement. She wagged her finger at the dog. "Do you understand, Harley? No naughty tricks, just good ones."

Dinner passed pleasantly enough. Shelley chatted about some of the pets who visited the vet clinic where she worked.

Ty talked about coaching Gracie's tee ball team and his plans to take some official coaching courses.

"Sounds like you made the right choice, staying here in Verona Lake once you retired from the game," Drew remarked.

Ty glanced at Shelley, who smiled back at him. "Yeah. I did."

Savannah's heart gave a little bump. Her sister had had some ups and downs in the romance department, but it looked like Shelley had at last found someone worthy of her. Still, it was hard not to worry…

Why? Are you just playing the protective big sister? Or maybe Shelley's right and you really don't trust men at all.

No. That wasn't true. Frowning, she helped herself to some potato salad she really didn't want and said "How long do you think you'll be staying in town, Drew?"

"Oh." He looked as though she'd caught him off guard. "Uh, I'm not sure. Just enjoying my down time here and taking each day as it comes."

Ty smirked. "Never thought I'd hear that from you. Seems like you always thrived on the pressure of a high-powered career."

Gracie seemed very concerned by Drew's reply. "But Harley's gonna stay with you, right? You won't give him back to the shelter?"

Drew shook his head. "Don't worry. Harley's safe with me. I won't let him down."

Gracie gave a big sigh of relief, then wiggled her eyebrows and sent him a conspiratorial smile.

Uh-oh. What was that about?

Before Savannah could probe further, Shelley announced "Plenty more sandwiches left. Drew, would you like another?"

"No, thanks. This was great. I'm full."

"Ty? Van? Should we wait a while for dessert? We've got brownies."

"I'm okay with waiting." Drew turned to Gracie. "We could take Harley for a walk. What do you think?"

"Yeah! Mom, you're gonna come too, right?"

"Why don't we clean up first, then we can all go," Savannah answered. Safety in numbers, after all.

"Ty and I can take care of this," Shelley responded oh-so-helpfully. "Why don't you three go on ahead?"

Savannah frowned, annoyed by her sister's obvious attempt at forcing her and Drew together.

"Come on, Mom!" Gracie cried.

There was no way to wriggle out of it gracefully. Savannah pinned on a smile. "Okay. Let's go."

Side by side they started down the path that wound around the park. Harley walked ahead of them while Drew held his leash.

"We still have to work on heel," he said.

"I see improvement, though," Savannah replied. "You've been putting a lot of work in with him."

"Trying to. He's keeping me busy, that's for sure."

"It must be hard getting used to Verona Lake, after living in the city. There's not much excitement here. Life's a lot slower paced."

"I don't know. Sometimes it's nice to enjoy a slower pace." He looked at her with warmth in his eyes. "Life here definitely has its charms."

His smile sent a shiver through her, making her glance away. *Get a grip, Savannah. A cute guy shows you some attention and you turn to mush? Pathetic.*

"Ty tells me you're a teacher," he went on, unaware of her inner struggle.

"Mom teaches fourth grade," Gracie put in. "She's always grading papers and stuff. She's got more homework than me!"

Drew gasped and goggled his eyes. "That much? Wow!"

Gracie giggled.

Addressing Savannah, he said "Sounds like you keep mighty busy yourself."

"No more than any other teacher. I enjoy it."

"My mom's a good teacher," Gracie said loyally.

"I'm sure she is."

The low timbre of his voice sent another thrill racing through her. Great. She pulled her jacket a bit tighter around her.

His face took on a look of concern. "Are you cold? We can cut this walk short."

Oh man, why did he have to be so darn attractive? Trying to hide her shiver, she answered. "Oh no. I'm fine."

Thankfully, Gracie was blissfully ignorant of her mom's discomfort. "Can I hold Harley's leash? Please?"

"He's pretty strong, hon. Better ask your mom."

"Mom, can I? Please? He's being good. See?"

If she hadn't been so flustered, Savannah might have responded differently. "Well, all right. For a little while. Be careful."

Drew handed Gracie the leash and she took it, beaming. Harley must have sensed the difference in tension because he glanced back at the people behind him.

"Good boy, Harley." Drew's voice held a warning note, as though reminding the dog to behave himself.

Harley made a soft huff and loped along at an easy pace. Easy enough for Savannah to let her guard down. Suddenly the dog stopped in his tracks and went still.

He made a strange sound, between a huff and a whimper, and stood tremblingly alert as his eyes fixed on something in the distance.

"What's he doing?" Gracie asked.

Drew didn't seem to know, either. "Harley."

That same instant, Harley took off running, tearing at the leash so forcefully he ripped it out of Gracie's hand. She stumbled, and only Drew's quick instincts kept her from falling. He grabbed her around the waist before she hit the ground face first. Harley raced off, the leash flying behind him.

"Gracie, are you all right?" Savannah cried.

Unconcerned for herself, Gracie tried to struggle free of Drew's grasp. "He ran away!"

"It's all right," Drew said. "We'll find him."

But the dog was already out of sight.

CHAPTER 10

Harley

I am so happy to see my friend Gracie again. It is fun to play with her and show her how I do Sit and Stay. It is still hard not to wiggle and move when Drew tells me Stay. I want to prance and lick Gracie because I love her so much. But I try to remember to be a Good Dog like my friends Boots and Zeno say.

Gracie holds my leash and we have fun on our walk when a familiar smell tickles my nose. I stop and stand very still to breathe it in again. It smells like cigars and old boots. I feel funny and trembly inside and all of a sudden I must run run run! I jerk the leash free and my legs run fast. Up ahead I see the man I used to live with. He was my person until I went away to Happy Hearts and the big room full of dog cages.

My nose was right!

My happy heart is full of joy and my tail goes round and round as I jump up and bark. *"Hello, hello! How are you? Where have you been? I missed you very much!"*

But he doesn't smile at me. He doesn't pet me or say "Hi,

Harley!" Instead, he frowns and tugs at the leash of a little dog at his feet.

The dog has short fur and pointy ears and little pointy teeth. He shows them when he growls at me, even though I try to make friends.

"Hello," I tell him. "My name is Harley and this man is my friend. I used to live with him."

The little dog snarls. "He is not your friend! He is my friend and he belongs to me! You are a Bad Dog and if you don't get away from us, I will bite you!"

Why is he so mean? I am not trying to hurt him. "I just want to say hello. I have not seen him for a long time."

"He doesn't like you anymore. You were Bad so he gave you away. He only likes me now so go away! I will bite you and eat you up!"

I whimper and back away. What a mean thing to say. He is little and I don't think he could eat me all up, but maybe he could eat a tiny bit of me. His teeth look very sharp.

The man snatches up the little dog in his arms. His face twists into a scary angry mask. Why isn't he glad to see me? Doesn't he remember me?

He kicks out at me with his foot and I scramble away. "Get away from us, Harley! Stupid mutt. Get lost."

He knows my name. He *does* remember me. But he is being very mean. I tremble and my heart feels sad and old, like a chew toy with no squeak left inside.

Soon Drew, Gracie, and Mom run up. Drew catches my leash and talks to the other man, who says things like "trouble" and "mutt" while Gracie strokes my head. I love Gracie. She is nice to me and never says mean things.

The man I used to live with does not like me anymore. When he turns away, the little dog yaps "Ha ha, Bad Dog! My man will never want you back because he has me now and I am better than you!"

I whimper and lean against Gracie. Will she still love me now that she knows I was Bad?

CHAPTER 11

Savannah

Harley hadn't gone far after all. They found him farther ahead on the path, circling and pawing at a man who held a small Chihuahua in his arms. The little dog yapped while the man kicked out at the Black Lab, hollering "Get away from us, Harley! Stupid mutt. Get lost."

Drew rushed forward and grabbed the end of Harley's leash, pulling him back. "Sorry. He got away from us."

"Yeah, he's always been trouble," the man grumbled.

"You…you called him by name. You know this dog?"

"You bet I know him." The man's mouth twisted into an ugly frown. "I used to own the stupid thing. He was nothing but a pain in the neck, always running away and causing trouble with the neighbors." He snuggled the Chihuahua. "You're not like that, are you, Cuddles?"

Cuddles ignored the man to yip sharply at Harley, who whimpered and cowered back against Drew.

"Smartest thing I ever did was get rid of that dumb dog," the man said. "You got him now, mister? Well, it won't be for long. Trust me. That dog's got problems."

"Maybe you're the problem," Drew said.

The man gave a snort of disgust and turned his back on them, to walk away in the other direction. "Come on, Cuddles. Let's get away from that mutt."

Harley whined as the man left. Then he looked at Drew, Gracie, and Savannah with big sad eyes, as though asking *What happened?*

Gracie, her eyes narrowed and her mouth tight, spoke first. "I *hate* him."

"Gracie, don't say hate," Savannah answered reflexively.

"I don't care. That man's mean. He called Harley a thing." She stroked Harley's soft ears. The dog gazed at her as though he still couldn't understand what was going on. "You're not a thing. You're a nice dog."

"Harley must have seen him before we did. Remembered, and wanted to—" Drew looked down and patted the dog's head sympathetically. "Wanted to say hello, I guess. Poor guy."

Savannah too felt moved to sympathy by Harley's plight. The dog held no grudge at being surrendered to the animal shelter. He wasn't angry at his former owner. He remembered the man with love and wanted to greet him joyfully. The man's angry response only hurt and confused him.

Wow. You're taking a pretty deep dive into Harley's psyche, aren't you? What are you, some kind of dog whisperer?

No. But she wasn't heartless, either.

Be careful, or you're going to end up as attached to Harley as Gracie is.

She held back a sigh. There was no doubt as to her daughter's feelings toward the big Black Lab. The more she saw of him, the fonder she grew. And yet, refusing to let Gracie spend time with him would only break her heart.

As a mom, Savannah was between a rock and a hard place.

"Harley's sad." Gracie looked on the verge of tears herself.

"He's all right," Savannah told her. "He's with people who like him now."

Gracie looked up, her eyes wide, her gaze intent. "Do *you* like him, Mom?"

Savannah wondered if she was walking into a trap. "Of course, I do." That was true. Just because she couldn't take him home didn't mean she disliked him. "He's a nice dog. He wants to please. He just makes mistakes."

"Everybody makes mistakes," Gracie reminded her.

"That's right."

"You know what? Let's cheer him up," Drew said.

Gracie's features crumpled in an expression of puzzlement. "How do we do that?"

"We give him a chance to be a good boy and remind him how smart he is."

Her face lit up with understanding. "Like when he sits."

As though he understood the word, though it wasn't spoken as a command, Harley planted his bottom on the ground. They laughed.

"Good boy, Harley! Can I give him one of those chicken cookies?"

Drew handed her a cookie morsel. "Do it like I showed you."

The dog sat patiently as Gracie closed her fist around the treat and lifted her hand over his head. When she released the goodie, he caught it in his mouth. "Good boy. See, you *are* smart."

Harley stood, preening at the compliment.

Drew said, "Let me show you something else we've been working on." Bending forward, he extended his right hand. "Harley, shake."

Harley gazed at the hand, then up at Drew's face.

"Come on, guy, we practiced this. Shake."

"Show him a cookie," Gracie suggested.

Drew took one from his pocket, holding it in his left hand. "Here. Come on, you remember. Shake."

Harley sat and gazed up at Drew hopefully.

Drew glanced at Savannah and Gracie and shrugged. "Well, like I said, we're still working on it."

Harley watched Drew and, as though a light bulb turned on in his head, pawed at his extended hand. Drew caught it and gave it a brief shake. "That's right. Good boy, Harley. Good shake."

Gracie and Savannah laughed and applauded as Harley gulped down his reward.

"Do it again!" Gracie cried. "Wait! Can I do it?"

"Sure. Come here."

She hurried over to face the dog. Drew gave her a bit of cookie. Reaching out with an open palm, she spoke softly and encouragingly. "Come on, Harley. You can do it. Shake."

The dog lifted his paw and placed it in her hand. Gracie held it and shook. "Good boy, Harley."

"Tell him 'good shake,'" Drew said.

"That's a good shake," Gracie repeated, releasing his paw and giving him the treat. She giggled when the dog licked her hand. "That tickles. You're a good smarty." Then she glanced at Savannah. "Mom, come on. You do it, too."

Savannah froze, suddenly on the spot. "Really?"

"Give it a try," Drew told her.

"Yeah, come on," Gracie urged.

Feeling foolishly nervous, she approached Harley. She didn't feel the same connection to him that her daughter and Drew seemed to. The dog's big brown eyes gazed at her eagerly. He glanced at her hands as though asking *"Where's my treat?"*

"Take a cookie," Gracie said.

Drew gave Savannah a crumbled piece of chicken-flavored snack. She bent forward and offered the dog her hand. "Harley. Shake?"

Harley raised his paw and plopped it on her palm. Savannah smiled, ridiculously proud of herself—and of Harley—and shook his paw. She then gave him the cookie, which disappeared in a blink.

"Good boy," she told him, stroking his head. He gave her a big doggy grin.

Gracie clapped her hands. "See, Mom? Isn't he smart?"

"Yes, he is." Harley gazed at her so trustingly that a wave of guilt swept over her. She couldn't give him the home he needed, no matter how Gracie wished otherwise.

For all the reasons you've explained to her. So don't weaken now. Hold the line.

The look on her daughter's face wasn't that different from Harley's—trusting and hopeful. Even Drew looked expectant. Then she understood that this afternoon's picnic wasn't just about showing off Harley's training. Gracie was hoping this display would get her mother to change her mind about the dog.

Well, time to gently but firmly squelch that plan.

"He's smart. A nice dog, too. Isn't it wonderful that Mr. Woodson has given him such a good home?"

Gracie's face fell in disappointment. "But Mom—"

Savannah cut her off. "It's getting a little late now. We should head back for dessert. Aunt Shelley and Ty will be waiting."

Her daughter's lower lip jutted out mutinously, but she didn't argue. Their walk back to the picnic area was a silent one.

After munching a brownie, Gracie was in a better mood. While she showed Ty and Shelley how Harley could sit and shake hands, Savannah had a private word with Drew.

"I've explained to Gracie over and over why we can't

bring Harley home. It looks like she still wants to convince me that we should adopt him."

Drew nodded. "Yeah. She, uh, kind of wanted me to go along with that little plan of hers." Flushing, he gave her an apologetic smile. "Sorry."

Savannah gave a small laugh. "I'm not surprised. My daughter can be quite stubborn when she's got her heart set on something."

"She can be pretty convincing, too. You might have a budding lawyer on your hands."

"I wouldn't mind that." Feeling suddenly shy, she said "I do appreciate your letting her visit with Harley. I'm sure you have a lot of other things you could do with your time."

"No." His brief, sincere response made her heart give a little jump. His gaze held hers. "I can't think of anything I'd rather be doing. It's been a good day. For Harley and for me." Glancing at Gracie, he added "I like seeing her smile."

Savannah eyed him as he watched Gracie. A tiny leaf had landed on his shoulder. Her fingers itched to brush it away, but she didn't dare. The navy-blue wool of his sweater looked soft, but not as soft as his dark brown hair, mussed by the breeze. She imagined her hand straying from his shoulder to his hair. How would it feel—smooth or coarse or springy?

Heat rushed through her, setting her cheeks on fire. *Think about something else.*

To banish temptation, she folded her hands tightly in her lap and looked away.

Her doubts came rushing back. "I'm still not sure it's a good idea. The more she sees him, the more attached she gets —and the harder it will be to let go."

"She was attached the first time she saw him. Why fight it? As far as I'm concerned, she's good for Harley. He needs to be socialized and spend time with adults and kids. And I think he's good for her. I mean, look at her. Ty mentioned she's kind of shy, but she's not shy now, is she? The way she's showing off Harley's tricks, it's building up her confidence. The way I see it, they're helping each other."

"But fostering is just a temporary thing," Savannah countered. "What happens when you decide to leave town? What's that mean for Gracie? And for Harley?"

"Harley won't go back to the shelter, that's for sure." Drew's voice was determined—even grim. "He's going to get a good home. I'll see to that."

"But it won't be *your* home. You're not staying in Verona Lake permanently. Gracie won't be able to see Harley in that new home, wherever it is. What then?"

His eyebrows lowered as his forehead crumpled. "You can't protect your daughter from ever getting hurt."

"I have to try. I'm her mom."

"But getting hurt is the chance we all take when we love something—or someone. What's the alternative?"

Taken aback, Savannah sucked in a sharp breath. His response left her speechless. She wanted to protect Gracie, not limit her.

Shelley's earlier words came back to her: *"You've got a wall. And you won't let anyone through."*

Was she trying to build a wall around Gracie, too?

The thought chilled her.

She didn't want to be one of those helicopter parents that constantly intervened in their child's life, stunting their independence and maturity. She couldn't protect her daughter from every disappointment in life.

"Why borrow trouble when neither one of us can predict the future?" Drew went on. "As far as I'm concerned, Gracie can visit Harley whenever she wants. It doesn't seem right to keep them apart when they're so crazy about each other."

Savannah didn't know how to answer. She'd felt so sure

in her stand just a little while ago but seeing how much Gracie had come out of her shell with Harley made her pause. Maybe what Drew was saying made sense…

Is it really Gracie you're worried about? Or maybe you're afraid you're the one who'll get too attached.

She didn't have long to ponder that because Gracie suddenly called to them. "Hey, Mom! Mr. Woodson! You see how good Harley's being?"

"You bet!" Drew stood and walked over to the pair. "You're doing a great job with him, honey."

Savannah trailed behind, feeling a bit woozy, buffeted by conflicting emotions. "I think it's about time for us to head home."

Gracie's face fell into a disappointed scowl. "Already? I want to play more with Harley." She wrapped her arms around the dog's neck.

Harley whimpered.

"See?" Gracie said. "He wants me to stay, too."

"I think he's uncomfortable with you grabbing his neck like that," Savannah answered.

Her daughter immediately released him. "Sorry, Harley."

"We've had a nice day. A picnic and a good walk with Harley. Let's not spoil it with an argument now. Come on." Savannah spoke firmly, hoping she wouldn't have to bust out her "mean mom" voice.

But before Gracie could dig in her heels, Drew spoke. "You know, animals are pretty sensitive to people. Especially dogs. They pick up on our emotions and take their cues from us."

Gracie eyed him in puzzlement. "What's that mean?"

"It means if you're upset, Harley will get upset, too. If you feel sad, so will he. We're trying to teach Harley to be a good dog, right? To listen to us and obey. That means we should set a good example for him."

Gracie thought this over for a bit. "So, I should like be good and do what my mom says? That will show Harley how to be good, too?"

Drew nodded. "That's right," he said quietly.

After puzzling it out a bit more she answered, "All right."

He smiled. "Good girl."

Gracie's face glowed with pride at Drew's compliment.

Wow. Savannah was impressed, even a bit jealous at how easily Drew handled the situation. There was no pouting, no whining, no dragging of feet. He really *was* good with Gracie.

At that moment, Savannah's gaze met Shelley's. Her sister raised an eyebrow and gave her a knowing look, as though saying *Didn't I tell you?*

Then Drew clapped his hands. "This was great, everybody. Tell you what, let's do it again. Next Saturday, my place. What do you say?"

Ty and Shelley exchanged a look. Ty shrugged. "Sounds good to me."

"Me, too," Shelley said. "It'll be fun."

"Yay," Gracie cried, hopping with excitement. "We can go too, right Mom?"

Savannah felt cornered. "Well, we'll see."

Her daughter's mouth screwed into a frown. "No fair. You always say 'we'll see' and it turns out to mean no."

"Well…" why was she hesitating? *It's not Gracie you're worried about. You don't trust yourself around this man. He's got you feeling all kinds of things. Things you haven't felt since—*

Four pairs of eyes—no, five, including Harley's— were watching her, waiting for her answer. She didn't want to be the party pooper, the Debbie Downer who spoiled everyone's fun. Besides, she and Drew wouldn't be alone, for goodness' sake. Ty and Shelley would be there, not to mention Gracie and Harley.

"All right." She smiled, not wanting to look like a crab.

She wasn't sure how convincing she was. "It sounds very nice. We'll go."

As Gracie whooped with happiness and told Harley goodbye, Savannah released a long slow exhale. She only hoped she wasn't making a huge mistake.

CHAPTER 12

Drew

Drew half-expected Savannah to call at the last minute and cancel their plans for the following Saturday. He was pleasantly surprised when she didn't. She and Gracie arrived at his place at two o'clock. He and Harley greeted them out front, Harley straining at his leash as soon as he saw Gracie running across the lawn toward him.

Drew reminded himself that in his role as dogfather, he needed to use every opportunity to train Harley and not let the dog's rambunctious nature get the best of him. "Harley. Sit."

The dog obeyed. Still, he wriggled with excitement.

Before the little girl could throw herself at Harley, Drew said "Gracie. Hold on. Let him settle down."

"Gracie, listen to Mr. Woodson," Savannah told her daughter. "We're trying to teach Harley to follow the rules, remember?"

Gracie came to a stop, biting her lip. Tamping down her natural exuberance was apparently as much a struggle for her as it was for Harley to control his.

Savannah trailed Gracie at a more measured pace. A stiff smile was fixed to her lips, as though she were politely determined to at least pretend she was glad to be here.

Harley, sitting at Drew's side, gave a little whine. His gaze moved from Gracie to Drew as he waited for a signal.

"Good sit, Harley," Drew said quietly, "All right, Gracie. You can come say hello."

Smiling, the little girl petted the dog's head, "Good boy, Harley."

"See if he remembers 'Shake'," Drew said.

She held out her hand. "Can you shake?"

Harley plopped his paw onto her palm and Gracie shook it. "Yay! Good boy!"

"Okay, Harley. Good boy." Drew released him from the command and Harley jumped to all fours, accepting Gracie's pats and praise with a doggy grin of delight.

Drew was heartened by the joyful connection of the goofy Lab and the little girl. He glanced at Gracie's mom. Her smile was no longer forced, but soft and genuine. He sensed she was just as touched by the scene as he was.

A tingling warmth spread through him. She was so lovely when she smiled.

But when she caught him looking at her, she retreated into cool formality. "Thank you for inviting us."

Her formality was catching. "I'm glad you could come." Then, realizing her sister wasn't with them: "Is Shelley coming later?"

Savannah shifted uncomfortably. "She got a call this morning from the clinic. The tech scheduled to go in today had an emergency, so they asked Shelley to sub. She won't be joining us."

"Oh. Sorry to hear that." Now he was doubly surprised that Savannah hadn't cancelled today, considering Shelley wasn't here to act as a buffer.

As though she could guess his thoughts, she said "Gracie's been looking forward to seeing Harley all week. I couldn't let her down."

So Harley was the only reason they'd shown up today. Drew felt a bit deflated to realize neither Gracie nor her mother was particularly interested in seeing *him*.

Savannah's face turned rosy with embarrassment and she hurried to add "Oh, I didn't mean—"

"It's all right," he said, laughing it off. "I'm just glad you're both here. As a matter of fact, Ty's not coming, either. He called and said something came up last minute. So it's just us three..." he glanced over at Gracie, who kneeled beside Harley and stroked him while he squirmed in pleasure. "Or, should I say, us four."

"Oh." The color drained from Savannah's cheeks as she took in the fact that there were no other adults present to act as quasi-chaperones.

To ease the awkward silence that descended, he said "Let's go around back. There's more room for Gracie and the dog to play."

He led them through the house, stopping to pick up a couple of tennis balls from the floor of the living room. "We can play a few games of fetch with him. It helps him work off some energy so he can focus better on training."

Harley's ears perked up the instant he saw the balls in Drew's hand. He was so intent on playing, he clunked into the glass door of the patio in his eagerness to get outside.

"Take it easy, guy." Drew slid open the door and slung a bright yellow ball. Harley raced for it as it arced across the sky.

When it landed on the grass, he snatched it up in his jaws and trotted over to Drew with his tail waving proudly.

Drew held out his hand to receive the ball. "Good boy, Harley. Drop it, now."

With the ball in his teeth, Harley thrust his head forward as though ready to give it over. Then he changed his mind and pranced away with a playful glint in his eye, as though saying *"You want it? Come and get it."*

Drew gave a rueful laugh. *That's what I get for trying to show off.* Embarrassment flashed through him—the kind of embarrassment he imagined a parent might feel for a glee-fully disobedient child.

Savannah pressed her lips tightly together, as though trying to hold back a smile.

"Harley, come on," Gracie cried, fisting her hands on her hips. "How can we play if you don't cooperate?"

Drew felt a flicker of surprise at her choice of words. Maybe she learned about cooperation from school, or from her mom. Either way, he was impressed. What a smart little girl.

"He's not being very cooperative, is he?" Drew said. "He's great at catching the ball. Just not so good at giving it back."

"He's smiling," Gracie observed. "He thinks it's fun to be naughty."

Drew threw the other ball, thinking it might distract Harley. When it landed, instead of dropping one ball to snatch up the other, the dog managed to get them both in his mouth. He trotted back to Drew and Gracie, proudly showing off his prizes.

"Harley, you're silly!" Gracie turned to her mother. "Mom, look what he did."

This time Savannah didn't try to hide her laughter. "Yes. I see."

Harley came just close enough to have Gracie reach out for a ball but scooted away before she could take one. Gracie ran a few steps after him. "Come on, no fair," she cried.

"Don't chase him, Gracie," Savannah said. To Drew she said, "May I make a suggestion?"

"Sure." At this point, what did he have to lose? Harley was doing a terrific job of making him look foolish.

"Well, I think Harley's looking for attention. Right now he's trying to get it by being naughty and disobeying commands. He wants us to chase him. But that would only reinforce his bad behavior. So what we should do now is just ignore him."

Gracie's small features squinched in confusion. "Ignore him?"

"That's right. Then he'll learn he can't get what he wants by disobeying. He'll only get our attention and praise when he does what he's supposed to."

"That's a great idea. Thanks." Drew grinned. "It's good to have a teacher around."

"Did you learn that in teacher school, Mom?" Gracie wanted to know.

"That and a few other things." Savannah gave her daughter a warm smile. "I also learned it being a parent."

A suspicious look crossed the little girl's face. "You mean you do that with me, too?" Something she'd apparently never considered.

"No comment," Savannah said airily.

While Gracie puzzled that out, Drew said "I stopped by the cider mill today and got some snacks. I'll get them and we can eat while Harley figures out we're not going to reward his bad behavior."

They sat around a table on the patio, snacking on apple cider and cinnamon donuts while Harley sat at a distance, still holding both tennis balls in his mouth. He watched them rather forlornly, as though wondering why no one wanted to play.

"Remember, we're ignoring him," Savannah reminded her daughter, who kept sneaking glances the dog's way. "Here, don't forget a napkin."

"Thank you," Gracie mumbled through a mouthful of donut.

"These are good, huh?" Drew said. "I picked them up at Fiedler's Farm. It's not far from here."

"We passed a sign for them on the road," Gracie piped up once she swallowed. "My friend Randi went on a hayride there with her moms. She said they have pumpkins there, too, and all kinds of stuff. Mom, can we get a pumpkin for Halloween?"

"We'll get one. Maybe not there, but someplace."

"Guess who I'm gonna be for Halloween? I'm gonna be Lightning Lass!" Gracie announced.

Drew had no idea who or what that was. "Is she someone from a comic book?"

"No, silly. She's on TV. She has superpowers and can shoot lightning from her fingertips. It can freeze the bad guys so they can't do any crimes. And she can make the lightning bolts twist into like ropes to tie them up."

"Wow. She sounds cool."

Gracie nodded. "She is. And she's got a friend named Zap who helps her."

Harley, perhaps tired of being ignored, chose that moment to trot up to them. He then pranced back and forth as though saying *"Hey, see what I got?"*

"Don't look at him," Drew murmured, though it was a struggle not to laugh at the dog's clowning. "Just ignore him."

When none of Harley's people gave him their attention, he tried something else. He crept up to Drew and nudged him with his nose. *Don't just sit there. Come on, chase me!*

When Drew didn't respond, Harley tried the same trick with Gracie. He gamboled away when a giggle escaped the little girl, then stopped and gazed at them in confusion when no one came after him.

Drew realized he wasn't the only one repressing laughter.

Gracie's lips were pinched tight and even Savannah looked as though she was struggling not to chuckle.

After another minute or two, the Black Lab slunk back near their table and sank onto the grass with a huff of surrender. *I give up. You people are no fun.*

Opening his mouth, he let the tennis balls drop onto the grass.

"Good boy, Harley," Drew said.

Harley's head popped up and his ears perked. *Huh? What did I do?*

Drew grabbed one of the balls and hurled it. The dog raced after it, caught it before it hit the ground and carried it back to him. When Drew held out his hand and said, "Drop it," Harley went still.

"Come on, guy. You know what to do," Drew told him.

The dog seemed to be waging an inner battle. His human expected him to do one thing, while his doggy impulse to play and be silly urged him to do the opposite.

"Please, Harley," Gracie pleaded softly. "Be a good boy."

That quiet little voice must have penetrated Harley's hard noggin, and his love for Gracie overcame everything. After a bit more hesitation, the dog loosened his jaws and let Drew take the ball.

Gracie clapped her hands. "Yay, Harley."

"Good boy." A rush of satisfaction filled Drew and he immediately wanted to laugh at himself. You'd think he was a proud parent, busting his buttons at his kid's accomplishment.

He's just a silly dog, for gosh sakes.

Just the same, there was something about Harley. Maybe it was the way he was so eager to please. Even when he was acting up, it wasn't out of meanness. He just wanted to have fun, and wanted his humans to have fun, too. You just couldn't help but love the crazy guy.

Love? That's going a bit too far, don't you think?

For sure. This fostering gig was just temporary. With any luck, Harley would find a permanent home with Gracie and her mom. That was the plan. They just had to get Savannah to agree.

But he had to admit, when it was time to say goodbye, he'd miss having ol' Harley around.

He fisted the tennis ball, giving it an extra squeeze as he pictured that goodbye. Then he glanced at Gracie, who eyed him expectantly.

"Can I throw it for him this time?"

He smiled, tossing her the ball. "Absolutely."

Harley's entire focus was concentrated on that ball as it flipped from Drew's hand to Gracie's, and he was already racing to capture it as she threw. Of course, she couldn't throw it as far as Drew did, but the dog didn't care. He leaped and caught the ball midair then trotted back to Gracie, pausing only a moment before dropping it at her feet.

Her mouth fell open as she goggled at Harley, then at Drew. "Did you see that? I didn't even tell him to drop it."

"Yeah," Drew uttered, just as amazed as she was. Would this crazy dog ever stop surprising him?

"Good dog!" The little girl cried, rubbing Harley between the ears while he gazed at her adoringly. Then he pranced in a little circle, like a show dog preening for an enraptured audience.

That led to them playing fetch and taking turns tossing the ball to Harley. Savannah sat watching until Gracie waved her over. "Come on, Mom! Come play with us."

Savannah approached them rather hesitantly. "I've never had much of an arm for throwing."

"That's not important," Drew told her, hoping to put her at ease. "We're just having fun." He tossed her the ball, which she fumbled. It slipped from her grasp, fell to the ground, and bounced once into Harley's mouth. He let it drop, then looked at Savannah as though confused. *What was that?*

She laughed, her face turning red. "Not much good at catching, either."

"Don't feel bad," Gracie said. "I'm not a good thrower, either."

That only made Savannah laugh harder. She took a deep breath and straightened her shoulders. "Okay, Harley. Let's try this again."

She tossed the ball underhand a short way and Harley took no time at all to retrieve it, drop it at her feet and look up at her expectantly. *Let's do it again!*

After that, Savannah fell easily into the game. They took turns tossing the ball to each other, then throwing it for Harley to catch. Drew enjoyed watching Savannah loosen up, smile and forget herself. When she relaxed, she seemed young and carefree, nothing like the stiff and formal school-teacher. She wasn't afraid to look a little silly. He very much liked—and felt quite drawn to—this side of her.

After a time, she shook her head no when the dog dropped the tennis ball at her feet. "No. Sorry, boy. That's it for today. Gracie, we should be getting home now."

Gracie's face fell and she groaned. "Aw, do we have to?"

"Yes. It's getting close to dinner time, and we need to get back."

Drew wanted to groan right along with Gracie. He didn't want them to go. The evening ahead loomed boring and dull without Gracie and her funny little way of saying whatever was on her mind. Without Savannah and her lovely smile. Even Harley seemed unhappy at the prospect of their leaving. He whimpered softly in disappointment when no one moved to toss the ball.

Drew heard himself ask "Do you have plans?"

Caught off guard, Savannah stuttered. "W-well, we...not exactly, but I'm sure you—"

"Not at all, no," he hurried on. "Look, why don't I order some pizza and we can have dinner here? Then after, we can check out the pumpkins at Fiedler's Farm and maybe even go on one of those hayrides. What do you say?"

Gracie hopped up and down. "Yes! Please, can we, Mom?"

Drew winced internally, wondering if he'd spoken too soon. Had he messed up once again and put Savannah in a spot, forcing her to be the bad guy if she said no?

Thankfully, she wasn't upset. In fact, she smiled as though she too didn't want the day to end. "That would be fun. Thank you."

CHAPTER 13

Savannah

"Can Harley come, too?" Gracie asked after they'd finished their pizza dinner and were getting ready to visit Fiedler's Farm.

Drew shook his head and smiled. "No, I think we better leave him here."

Gracie looked mildly disappointed but didn't argue. "We'll get a pumpkin for you, too," she told the dog, who pranced as though excited by the prospect of getting his very own pumpkin.

At the farm, there were plenty of pumpkins on display as well as gourds in funny shapes, multicolored ears of corn, and apples of every variety. Gracie watched in fascination as the cider press was demonstrated. After much deliberation, she selected two little pumpkins. "One's for me, the other's for Harley," she announced. "They match."

Savannah hadn't intended to get a pumpkin, but suddenly inspired by the holiday surroundings she decided to buy a medium sized one for their doorstep. "If Mr. Russo says it's all right."

"Are you getting one, too?" Gracie asked Drew, who shrugged.

"You think I should?"

"Yes! A big one."

"Okay. You help me pick one out, all right?"

Savannah watched fondly as her daughter took her job as assistant pumpkin selector most seriously. She nixed all the pumpkins that looked lopsided or weren't properly round or brightly colored enough.

"Here. This one," Gracie announced, pointing at a very large, round, orange pumpkin.

Drew knitted his brow as though the two of them were making an Extremely Important Decision. "You're sure, now?"

She nodded emphatically. "Yes."

"All right, then. Oof." Lifting it, he pretended to stagger under its weight. Gracie giggled. "It's a big one, all right."

As they carried their selections to the checkout counter, Savannah marveled at the easy connection between her daughter and Drew. He made her laugh and at the same time, treated her with the respect he'd show a friend, never speaking down to her or treating her like "just a kid."

Watching the way he related to Gracie gave Savannah a great feeling of tenderness.

That was troublesome. It would be foolish to develop feelings for a man just because he was kind to her child.

But maybe, for now, she wouldn't worry about it.

As they prepared to pay for their purchases, the counter man said "Our Haunted Hayride will be starting in a few minutes. We have a few seats left. Would you folks like to join us?"

Gracie's eyes lit up. Savannah went into Mom Mode. "How scary is it? Too scary for a six-year-old?" she asked. If any zombies or chainsaw killers were to appear, her answer would be a hard no.

The man smiled understandingly. "It's very family friendly. Our grown-up version starts at ten o'clock."

Savannah knew Gracie was holding her breath, waiting for her decision. From the looks of him, Drew was doing much the same thing. She couldn't let them down. "May we have three tickets? Two adults and one child."

Drew insisted on paying for all their tickets and the pumpkins.

"You can leave your pumpkins here, behind the counter, and pick them up at the end of the ride," the counter man told them.

"I want to keep mine," Gracie said, holding on to her little pumpkin.

They climbed up into a large wagon with hay spread on the bottom and square bales set up along the perimeter. The three of them perched on a large bale as the tractor pulling the wagon started to growl.

Gracie sneezed. "This hay tickles my nose."

Savannah draped her arm around her daughter's shoulder as Gracie snuggled closer, her pumpkin on her lap. "Are you cold?"

Gracie shook her head. "No."

"There's a blanket here if you want one," Drew said from Savannah's other side. She was sandwiched between them with Gracie's head nestled on one shoulder, while her other shoulder pressed against Drew's. Sharing one seat had them squeezed quite close and Savannah couldn't deny the warmth flooding her at his nearness.

"I think we're good for now," she murmured.

Dusk descended upon them. The blazing oranges and pinks of sunset had quieted into a mid-blue. As the wagon rattled along, they passed a cackling, green-faced witch stirring her "witches' brew" in a cauldron, which turned out to be applesauce. As the sky darkened, they rumbled into a cornfield where a "scarecrow" shivered and shook, then descended from its pole to do a funny little dance.

Each bump of the wagon nudged her closer to Drew, sending little sparks of awareness through her. She tried to put a bit of distance between them when the wagon pulled into a Quonsett hut open on both ends, forming a tunnel. Spooky music was rigged to play in the pitch-black darkness. The only light came from the grinning neon orange pumpkins painted on the walls of the hut.

Something suddenly descended from the ceiling, bouncing in front of Savannah, making her jump. She let out a yelp and without thinking, grabbed Drew's arm, digging her fingers into his sleeve.

The something turned out to be a large papier mache spider with a smiley face, googly eyes and eight legs that wiggled and danced. Others on the ride chuckled at the spider and Savannah's reaction to it. When she collected herself, she joined in the laughter.

"Were you scared, Mom?" Gracie asked, wide-eyed.

"Not really," Savannah answered, her face glowing with embarrassment. "Just startled, I guess."

Then she realized she was still clutching Drew's arm, which made her face even hotter. Just as she was about to let go, he placed his hand over hers. And kept it there.

His touch sent warmth and contentment flowing through her as the tractor again growled and the wagon rattled out of the man-made tunnel. The sky was inky now and stars glittered overhead. With Gracie nestled against her and Drew's hand lightly holding hers, Savannah took a deep breath of the crisp air and allowed herself to dream.

If only...

If only this evening might never end.

If only she and Gracie didn't have to say goodbye to Drew at evening's end.

If only the three of them were a real family.

CHAPTER 14

Harley

"Stop squirming," my friend Drew tells me. "Be good so I can get this thing fastened."

He is putting a floppy cloth thing on me and tying it around my neck. I try to stand still and be Good, but I do not like this bad thing on me.

"You want Gracie to be surprised, don't you?" He finishes tying the thing and stands, looking me over from nose to tail. "She's going to love your costume."

Gracie? Am I going to see her tonight? My tail goes round and round in joy and my bouncy heart does a triple bounce. I love my friend Gracie. I will even wear this costume that feels very strange if it will make her happy.

I was very sad that day in the park when my used-to-be person and his little dog with the sharp teeth said I was Bad. But Gracie didn't listen to them. She still likes me and thinks I am Good. That is why I will always be her friend.

"Let's go," Drew says. We leave the house and go to the car. He opens the door so I can jump in the back seat. He even opens the window so I can stick out my head and let the wind flap in my ears. That is fun.

When the car stops, we get out and meet Gracie and the lady named Mom in front of their house. I know it is Gracie because of her smell, but she looks different. She has something over her eyes with two holes to see through and a red shirt with a bright gold slash on it. She has a floppy cloth around her neck just like me.

I give a glad woof when she hugs me. "Harley! You're dressed like Zap! Now we match!"

I don't know what that means or what a Zap is, but it feels good to make her happy.

My friend Drew laughs. "When you told me you were dressing up as Lightning Lass for Halloween, I did a little research."

"Did you watch the show?" Gracie asks.

"I did. And I thought you needed a sidekick like she has. So did Harley. He volunteered to come along as Zap."

I don't understand. A sidekick? I would never kick Gracie in the side, and she would never kick me. Kicking is mean.

Then she tells me "We're superheroes, Harley. Just like on TV. I'm Lightning Lass and you're my faithful friend Zap. See, we even have the same lightning bolts on our costumes. We fight bad guys."

My chest fills with pride. Now I understand. Gracie and I are heroes. Heroes are Good. They help people and save the day.

Gracie looks at Mom. "Did you know he was going to be Zap?"

Mom shakes her head. "Drew told me he had a surprise for us, but I didn't know it was this. You look very handsome, Harley."

My tail flaps back and forth as a warm feeling glows inside me. I am glad Mom likes me. She is a nice lady.

Gracie carries a big bag and says "Trick or Treat" as the four of us go from door to door along the street. There are others out too, in scary witch masks and monster faces, but I know from their smell that they are just children dressing up. The children are dressed as clowns, pirates, superheroes, and lots of other things. Grownups trail behind, waiting as the boys and girls get their treats. I am not even the only dog out tonight. We pass a little dachshund who is wearing a hot dog bun outfit, and a poodle dressed in a poofy pink skirt and bow. When we pass a Golden Retriever wearing a halo over his head, he barks "Cool costume, dude."

I prance and say "Thank you! Yours is nice, too."

Mom and Drew wait for us on the sidewalk while we go up to a house with the porch light on. On our way, Gracie whispers a secret to me.

"I think Mr. Woodson and my mom like each other, don't you? Wouldn't it be great if they got married? Then you and me could always be together."

Yes, yes! I want to be with my friend Gracie always. I want to be with Drew and Mom, too.

"If we spend lots of time together, maybe they'll fall in love and get married? Isn't that a good plan? I'll make sure Mom lets me see you a lot. But you need to help. You need to be a really good boy. Okay?"

Yes! This is a good plan. I will try so hard to be Good if it means we can all be a family.

When Gracie and I reach the door, it opens and Gracie cries "Trick or Treat!"

But something Bad happens! Instead of a person, a big hairy Thing stands there, roaring and thumping its chest.

Gracie gives a surprised little cry and the grownups behind us laugh, but I do not think this is funny. This Bad Thing is trying to scare my friend!

I will not let him hurt her. I must be a hero and protect

her. I push in front of her to keep him away and bark very loud. *"Go away, you Bad Thing! Do not scare my friend Gracie! You are mean!"*

The Thing has black fur all over except for its hands and face. It has strange little eyes and two holes for a nose. And it talks! "Take it easy, doggie. I'm just having a little fun." Then it pulls off its head and there is a man inside!

Gracie laughs and I bark louder, very confused. What is happening? Did the Thing eat the man?

Gracie strokes my head. "It's all right, Harley. Don't be scared. He's just wearing a costume."

Oh. He is just dressed up and playing make-believe, like Gracie and the other children and me. She says he is just pretending to be a grilla.

I have never seen a grilla before but I don't think I like them. They are too hairy and big. But the man is nice. He gives Gracie some treats and even puts a dog biscuit in her bag for me.

"Thank you," she says. Then she looks at Mom. "Did you see what Harley did? He thought the man in the costume was a real gorilla. He wanted to protect me."

Mom nods and smiles. "Yes."

"That was brave of you, Harley." Gracie pets me and looks at me with eyes full of love. I love her, too. "You're a good dog."

Good Dog. Those are the happiest words in the whole world. I always want to be a Good Dog for Gracie. I want our plan to work because it is sad when we have to say goodbye.

I am going to try very hard to be Good.

CHAPTER 15

Drew

At the end of the evening, they took the short walk home. Gracie's bulging treat bag bumped against her side. "Can I have some candy when I get home? Harley wants his dog treat, too."

"Yes, you can both have a treat," Savannah answered. "But then I'll hold on to the bag so you don't make yourself sick. Oh, Mr. and Mrs. Russo want you to stop by and show them your costume. They said they have something special for you, too."

Gracie could barely control her excitement. "Oh, boy! Can I go now?"

Since they were in spotting distance of the door, Savannah gave the go-ahead. "All right."

"Can I bring Harley? I want to show them his costume, too."

"No, he better stay with me," her mother answered. "Tomorrow we can show them the picture we took of you and Zap."

Only mildly disappointed, Gracie gave Harley a pat on

the head, then scurried up to the Russo's front door and knocked. A moment later she stepped inside.

Drew couldn't help but laugh at the little girl's enthusiasm. "Kids and candy, huh?"

Savannah smiled. "That's right. No matter how you try to sell them on the virtues of fruits and veggies, chocolate bars and sour gummies win out every time."

"Well, they're not dumb." Changing the subject slightly, he observed "It's nice that your landlords take an interest in Gracie."

"It is. Their grandkids are older and live out of state, so they don't see them too often. They've taken Gracie under their wing as a kind of 'adopted' granddaughter. They've been very kind."

"Does she see much of her real grandma and grandpa?"

Savannah hesitated for so long before answering that Drew realized, too late, he'd stepped onto dangerous ground. *Open mouth, insert foot.* "Forget I asked. I have a way of—"

"No, it's all right. The truth is, she doesn't know her grandparents because...well, I don't know where my parents are. I've never known my father and I lost track of my mother years ago. My sister and I grew up in foster care."

Drew's heart plummeted to the soles of his shoes. "My gosh...I'm sorry."

"It's okay. I mean, it wasn't great, but it wasn't terrible, either. Shelley and I always had each other. We were lucky that way. We were never separated."

"Thank heaven for that much," he murmured. Since he'd already messed up, he figured he might as well go all in. "What about Gracie's dad? His parents aren't involved either?"

Shaking her head, she looked away. "No. No more than her father is."

Anger flashed through him. What was wrong with those

people? How could anyone turn their back on a sweet little girl like Gracie? What kind of rotten, selfish souls were they?

No real man would turn his back on his own child.

"Their loss." He ground the words through his teeth. "If they're that stupid, they don't deserve her, anyway."

"Maybe I'm the stupid one," she answered.

That made him even angrier. "How can you say that? You're the best mother any child could have."

"Not really. Not such a great mom if I can't give my daughter a father."

It wrecked him, seeing her so sad and ashamed. *She* had nothing to blame herself for. The urge to sweep her into his arms was overwhelming. He resisted, but it was a mighty struggle. He only wanted to nestle her against him. Tell her how wonderful he thought she was. Hold her until she believed it too.

Instead, he took her hands. "I don't know what the story is, but if he's not in her life, that's on him. Not you. My dad bailed on me when I was a kid, so I know a little something about it. It was my mom who held it together. She raised me. Took care of me. And because of her, I never felt unloved. Later, when she remarried, my stepfather took on the role of dad, and I couldn't have asked for a better one.

"There's all kinds of families out there, you know? Some with one parent, some with stepparents, or with two moms, two dads. All kinds. And as long as a kid knows they're loved, they're gonna be all right."

"I know that's true," she answered. "But I grew up with no father, and I didn't want to repeat the cycle. I wanted things to be different for Gracie."

"They're already different," he insisted, enfolding her hands and bringing them up to his chest. "That little girl knows how much you love her. She's one lucky kid."

The glow of the streetlamp above them illuminated her

tremulous smile and the tears glistening in her eyes. "Thank you."

Her voice was soft and breathy. The urge to hold and comfort her flooded him again, pulling him in like an undertow. He couldn't resist...didn't even try.

He stepped in and placed his lips tenderly on hers.

That gentle touch of lips made the world spin like one of those circling camera shots in a movie. Along with the dizzying swirl came the fizz and pop of bubbly champagne as desire foamed through him. She was so lovely. So sweet and caring...

A whimper penetrated his daze, followed by a paw scratching at his pants leg. Harley stared up at them, his head tilted in confusion. *What are you two doing?*

Drew took a step back, and Savannah did the same. Bubbles still fizzed in his head, sending him off-kilter. Savannah looked dazed as well. Before he could speak—or even think what to say—Gracie burst from the Russo's door, waving a bag of treats.

"Mrs. Russo gave me some of her homemade popcorn balls, Mom. She said I should share them with you. Her and Mr. Russo really liked my costume and said I looked just like Lightning Lass. They know who she is cause their grandkids watch the show, too. I told them about Harley being Zap and they thought that was funny. Mom, can we make popcorn balls sometime? Maybe Mrs. Russo will show us how..."

Gracie showed no sign of slowing down, fueled either by the sugary treats she'd eaten or the excitement of Halloween night. Savannah, eyeing Drew hesitantly, seemed only vaguely aware of her daughter's ramblings.

"Yes, we'll ask her sometime," she murmured, gently shushing her daughter. "But you've got lots of treats now and everyone's seen your costume. It's time to say goodnight and go inside."

"And Harley should be getting home, too," Drew added to forestall any arguments from Gracie. "Superheroes need their beauty sleep so they can wake up ready to save the world."

"Beauty sleep?" Gracie laughed. "But Harley's a boy dog. He's not beautiful. He's handsome."

In response, Harley lifted his head, as though showing off his handsome profile.

Drew tugged his leash. "Okay, guy. Let's go."

"Wait," Gracie cried. "His dog biscuit!"

She dug it out of her treat bag and handed it to Savannah, who gave it to Drew.

"Thanks," he murmured, holding her gaze. He wanted to say something but suddenly felt as tongue-tied as a kid on his first date. What could he say, anyway, with a big-eyed little girl watching them?

He hadn't planned that kiss. It had come out of nowhere, surprising him as much as it had Savannah. But he wasn't sorry. No way. And he'd trade a year of his life for another kiss just like that first one.

Savannah smiled at him, her gaze soft, as though she understood.

"I'll...talk to you soon." As far as he was concerned, it couldn't be soon enough.

She nodded. "Yes."

Drew led Harley away, pausing a moment to glance over his shoulder at Savannah and Gracie, who waved back at him. After he got Harley in the car, he sank into the driver's seat and slumped back. Once he got home, he'd have to fix an ice pack for his head. Or something. He felt that drunk.

He wondered how Savannah felt.

CHAPTER 16

Savannah

Half an hour later, Savannah's lips still tingled from Drew's kiss and her head still felt muzzy. Thankfully, Gracie didn't seem to notice as she got ready for bed.

"Hey, Mom?"

Savannah gathered up the cape, shirt and skirt her daughter had cast aside while changing into her pajamas. "Hmmm?"

"That was cool how Mr. Woodson dressed Harley up like Zap, wasn't it?"

"Uh-huh. Very cool." She pictured Drew's face, illuminated by the streetlight, as he lifted her hands to his chest.

Remembered the warmth of his body, so close to hers.

Relived the sweet sensation of his kiss as their lips met...

"Hey, Mom!" Gracie had finished buttoning her pajama top and was staring up at Savannah. "Didn't you hear I what I said?"

Oh, brother. Time to stop woolgathering and get her head back in the mom game. "Sorry. What was it?"

Gracie huffed impatiently. "I said, wasn't it brave of Harley to protect me when he thought it was a real gorilla?"

"Yes. Did you brush your teeth?"

"Oh. I forgot."

"Uh-huh." Tooth-brushing was a habit her daughter often conveniently "forgot." "Well, go do it now."

"Can I just have one more candy bar from my bag before I do? Those little mini ones hardly even count."

"You've had enough candy tonight. Go brush."

"Aww…" Gracie shuffled her feet trudging into the bathroom. Savannah followed to supervise. As her daughter brushed and rinsed, Savannah leaned against the door jamb and thought about the kiss.

What did it mean?

When Gracie finished, they returned to her bedroom to complete their bedtime routine. As she tucked her daughter in, Gracie had more to say.

"Mom, don't you think Mr. Woodson is a real nice man?"

"Of course, I do." A wave of suspicion traveled through her. She gave her daughter a narrow look. "Why do you ask?"

Ignoring the question, Gracie went on. "And he's handsome, too, isn't he?"

A tiny shiver passed over her. *Yes.* But instead of answering in the affirmative, she went for a prim little platitude. "There are many more important things about a person than his looks."

"I know. Like if he's good to people. And kind to animals. Mr. Woodson is real kind to Harley, isn't he?"

"Yes." Time to put an end to this one-track conversation. Savannah gave her daughter a goodnight kiss. "Now it's time to go to sleep. Sweet dreams."

Gracie yawned. "You'll leave the door open, won't you? Just a crack."

"Yes, I will. Just like always."

"Mom, can I tell you one more thing?" Gracie asked, blinking sleepily.

"What is it?"

"I like Mr. Woodson a lot, too."

Savannah smiled. "That's good to know. Good night."

"Night."

Savannah switched off the overhead light and made a foray into the kitchen. Gracie's treat bag lay on the counter. She snitched a mini candy bar before placing the bag in the cupboard.

In the living room, she flopped into an armchair. The candy wrapper crackled as she tore it open. Savannah bit into the treat and gave herself over to memories of Drew's kiss.

Like a candy bar, it had been as sweet as caramel and seductive as chocolate. And even more delicious.

Why had he kissed her? Had it only been an impulsive act of comfort, or something more?

And if it *was* more? How did that make her feel?

Confused. Frightened.

Hopeful.

CHAPTER 17

Drew

"Sorry, guy," Drew told Harley a few days later when the dog trailed him to the front door, prancing in excitement. "You can't come along this time."

He felt a bit guilty when Harley gave a disappointed whimper, but it couldn't be helped. He had something important to do and couldn't be distracted by the dog's antics.

He slid behind the wheel of his car and started the engine. If anyone saw the goofy smile on his face, they'd wonder if he'd been hit on the head. He didn't care. He'd felt this way since Halloween. When he'd kissed Savannah.

Ever since that kiss, he couldn't stop thinking about her.

She'd been so brave to share her past with him that night. She'd overcome a sad, painful experience to become a successful teacher and a great, loving mom. She wasn't angry or bitter. Her courage and perseverance left him humbled.

And got him thinking about his own life. If she could get over her past, maybe he could get over his.

He'd given it a lot of thought the past few days. Maybe it

was time to let go of his anger. Let go of the past. He'd never love Frank the way he loved Henry, his stepfather. The only real father Drew had ever known. But maybe, if they could start fresh, he and Frank could be something like friends.

That possibility lightened Drew's spirit, as though a weight had been lifted from him. He had Savannah to thank for that. Getting to know her and Gracie made him a better man.

But Savannah was more than a role model to him. She was a vibrant woman with a smile that lit up her face, a nose that crinkled when she laughed, and eyes that glowed with love every time she looked at her daughter. She smelled like sugar cookies and her lips tasted sweeter than chocolate fudge cake.

Yeah, he had it bad for her. Her funny little daughter had also captured his heart.

And he wanted more time with them. Time enough for to them feel sure of him. He was already sure of them. Though he'd come to Verona Lake thinking his stay would only be temporary, his plans were different now. All due to an amazing woman, her adorable little girl, and a big clown of a dog. They'd all made a home in his heart, and he couldn't picture life without them.

He was no longer biding time in Verona Lake. No longer felt an urge to return to the city and rejoin *All in the Game*. Money was no problem—he had plenty of it. He'd find ways to spend his days and stay useful. Maybe take up coaching like his friend Ty. Or get involved in philanthropy and fundraising—there were a lot of worthy causes he could get behind. Heck, maybe even start a business. He had all the time in the world to decide.

Getting a little ahead of yourself, aren't you, bud? Making a lot of plans without consulting Savannah. She's going to want to have a say in things, don't you think?

She was bound to have plenty to say. And that was just fine with him.

Drew was still grinning when he pulled into the lot at the Lakeside Court Motel. He never dreamed he'd feel this way about any woman. Be head over heels in love like those characters in movies or sappy TV shows. He'd always rolled his eyes at the concept. His past relationships had been fun, but never serious. He'd always held himself a bit distant, never giving his whole heart. Thinking if he kept it light, no one would get hurt. Now he wondered if he'd only been trying to protect himself.

When Drew didn't find Frank in his room, he decided to check out the pool area. The old guy seemed to like sitting there just watching traffic.

Pity washed through him. Imagine being so lonely that watching cars pass qualified as entertainment.

That's not your fault, though. The guy made his bed years ago. If he hadn't abandoned his family, he wouldn't be alone now.

True enough. And for years Drew had hated him for that abandonment. But seeing how Frank had messed up his life, Drew's perspective had changed. In the end, the man had only cheated himself.

You can let it go now. Just let the anger go and try to get past it.

As Drew approached the swimming pool, he saw that his guess was correct. Frank sat in a lawn chair facing the road and in fact, was not alone. Another much younger man had pulled up a chair next to him. The two were engrossed in conversation.

"What's this all about?" The young guy said. He wore jeans and a tee shirt. A blue bill cap covered his brown hair. "That's what I want to know. You told Mom and me you'd be out on a camping trip with some buddies. I knew that was bull from the jump. What buddies? And since when have you ever gone camping? Now I track you down here at some out of the way motel in Nowheresville."

"Does your mother know where I am?" Frank asked.

"Heck, no. I wasn't about to tell her a thing, not until I could talk to you myself. Make sure you weren't keeping some chick on the side."

Frank snorted. "You know me better than that, Cole. Your mother's the only woman for me."

"I thought I knew you, till you pulled this trick."

Drew stopped walking. Stopped breathing. Who was this Cole? No stranger, that was for sure. He and Frank knew each other well and obviously had a relationship. A close relationship, from the sound of it.

So why had Frank never mentioned him?

"How'd you find me, anyway?" Frank asked gruffly.

"Duh, dude. There's lots of apps for that. You geezers never think of that stuff."

"Crud."

"Yeah. So. What's going on?"

That's what I'd like to know. A burning sensation rose in Drew's chest as his vision blurred. All this time, he'd believed Frank was a pathetic, down on his luck loser. Friendless and alone, subsisting on the crumbs of goodwill doled out by Drew. The only thing keeping him out of the gutter.

Or maybe that's just what you wanted to believe. That Karma had finally meted out some justice to the coward who left you in the dust without a backward glance.

Cole went on. "Is this about that deal you've been going on about? All those hints about coming into money?"

A sickening chill shot through Drew. Money? Was that what Frank was after all along? Had he been playing the long con from the start?

Drew ground his teeth as tightness constricted his chest. He curled his fists. By gosh, he wanted answers. Deserved them. Why was he skulking back here, eavesdropping, as though he were ashamed to show his face?

He had *nothing* to be ashamed of.

He strode forward, ignoring Frank completely, and stood before the guy named Cole. "Hey. Drew Woodson." Flicking a glance at Frank, he added, "I'm his son."

Cole stood slowly, as though taking Drew's measure. He was younger than Drew had figured, in his late teens, maybe. Though he was as tall as Drew, he was whip thin and rangy. He hadn't yet filled out into the man he would become.

The brim of Cole's cap cast a shadow, obscuring his eyes. "Yeah. I know. So am I."

I know. So am I. Those words caused the acid burn in Drew's chest to foam up into his throat. He clenched his jaws to keep it from surging out. It took a moment to gain control, but he refused to show any weakness in front of these two men—one a stranger, the other a liar.

Gritting his teeth, he put on a shark's smile. "That puts you one up on me…Cole, is it? Frank conveniently forgot to tell me he had another kid."

"He's got a wife, too," Cole said, almost pugnaciously, as though daring Drew to argue.

So that was the "Mom" Cole had mentioned. *And the hits just keep on coming.* "No kidding. She know she's wifey number two?"

"Sure. Just like we knew about you. Dad never kept any secrets from us." A momentary look of uncertainty crossed his face. "Until now…"

"No secrets, huh? Wish I could make the same claim. Do me a favor, Cole, and fill me in. Tell me a little bit about yourself. About Frank, there. He's your dad for real? Not your stepfather?"

"Yeah, he's my real dad," Cole answered, his voice a sharp edge. "He and my mom have been together my whole life."

His whole life. And from the looks of him, Cole had to be about, what? Seventeen, eighteen?

"He was around the whole time? In the same house? There every day?"

"Well, yeah." Now Cole sounded confused. "Well, when he was home."

Drew grabbed on to that detail like it was a life-preserver. "So he wasn't around all the time." Why was that so important to him? Why did it matter?

"How could he be," Cole said, "when he did over the road trucking? Sometimes he was away for days, driving his rig. But when he wasn't on the road, he was home with us. Mom and me."

That hit Drew like a punch in the gut, and the impact made him see double. Again, he fought the urge to be sick.

Frank had been a father to Cole, the father he'd never been to Drew. He'd been there for family dinners of meat loaf and mashed potatoes. For lazy Saturdays at the fishing hole, teaching his son how to bait a hook. For birthdays and Christmases and all the days in between.

Why Cole and not me? Why wasn't I good enough to stick around for?

When the pain subsided, Drew asked "What'd he tell you about me? About my mom?"

"Not much. We knew he'd been married before…" Cole's gaze slid away. "Had a kid…"

"Uh-huh. That makes us brothers. Half-brothers, anyway. So you never wondered about me? Knowing you had a brother out there in the world, someone you never met?"

"Sure, I wondered." Cole's voice was quiet.

"But you never asked him why? Why he never saw me? Never brought me around? Huh?"

Maybe you were scared to ask. Cause you didn't want to know.

"We figured he had his reasons…"

"Reasons. Yeah." Drew couldn't stop himself from battering the younger man with questions, even though he knew he was taking out his anger on the wrong person. What could Cole have done about it? He'd only been a kid himself. None of it was his fault.

Only one person was at fault, and he sat there as still as a stone, saying nothing.

Drew directed a withering look at Frank. If his eyes had been lasers, the old man would have been reduced to a pile of smoking ash.

"What *did* you tell them, Frank? That my mother was an evil hag who never let you see your beloved first-born?"

"No." Frank refused to look at him, a sure sign of guilt. "I never badmouthed your mom."

"Big of you," Drew said. "Guess you never mentioned how you disappeared on her one fine day, leaving her with no money and a snot nosed five-year-old to raise on her own. How she had to work two and sometimes three jobs just to keep a roof over our heads and food in our bellies. And how you never sent one dime to help out. Never called, never sent so much as a postcard to let her know how or where you were. Never bothered showing up in court when she divorced your useless behind. Never did a blasted thing."

Frank nodded, still not looking at him. "That's right. Not a thing."

A bark of laughter escaped Drew, scraping his throat. Was he supposed to be moved by this show of humility? Frank was an actor who could give those Academy Award winners a run for their money. He was a liar and a fake. Nothing he said or did could be believed.

Cole, on the other hand, looked shocked. His face had gone white. Even through his own sickening disappointment, Drew felt sorry for him.

"No. You just moved on and made a whole new family,

didn't you? Never wasted a minute looking back." Drew stared down at Frank, who still hadn't moved. He was beyond anger now. Beyond all feeling. He was simply numb. And tired. Too tired to play any more games.

"So all this stuff about wanting to get to know me, that was all a load, huh? What are you after, Frank? I asked you the first time we met if you were looking for money. You said no. But you know something? I'd have a lot more respect for you now if you'd just told me the truth. But you had to string me along, didn't you? Soften me up. Make sure I'd be an easy mark. Make me think that you really—"

That you really cared.

But he didn't say it. *Don't let him know. Don't let him see how much it hurts.*

He had to get out of here. Get away from these two before he cracked. "Okay, well, I'm out of here. Your room's paid up till the end of the week, Frank. After that, you're on your own. So act accordingly."

Hesitating, he spared a glance for Cole, who looked shaken. Torn between his image of the father he thought he knew and the one revealed to him today. In spite of his own anger and hurt, Drew felt bad for the kid. And felt the sting of loss, knowing he'd likely never see Cole again.

He's my brother. And he'll never be more than a stranger to me.

Nothing he could do about that. Setting his jaw, Drew strode to his car. Just as he tugged the door open, Frank called his name.

Heaven help him, Drew froze. Didn't know why. As much as he wanted to drive off and never see Frank's face again, a small part of him wanted to give the man one last chance. A chance to what, though? To apologize?

As though that could set things rights. Heck, a hundred apologies wouldn't be enough.

The old man was short of breath and puffing when he

reached Drew. "I didn't know he'd show up like this. Wanted you two to meet under different circumstances."

Yeah, right. "Well, you mucked that up real good, didn't you? Just like you did everything in your life."

"I mucked up lots of ways, but not when it came to Cole. He's a good kid. Smart, too. Does good in school. A good athlete."

Drew mouth twisted in a bitter grin. "Guess he takes after his mom, then. I can't picture he got anything worthwhile from you."

Frank plowed ahead as though Drew hadn't spoken. "He's graduating this year and would like to go to college. He doesn't say much about it—knows me and his mom can't afford to send him. He doesn't want to hurt us, especially his mother. She feels real bad we can't do more for him. So do I, but even with the wife working we've only ever scraped by paycheck to paycheck. There was never enough left over to put aside for any kind of college fund. But if I could give Cole the money to go to school, he could really make something of himself."

Drew could see the direction in which this conversation was headed. Though he wasn't surprised, he still felt a sickening, gut-twisting rage. "You mean if *I* gave him the money."

"He *is* your brother," Frank watched him intently, as though they were at a poker table and he was looking for any little sign of weakness.

"So you say." Frank had some stones, after walking out on him, to come asking for a handout. *Well, you wondered what brought him back. Now you know.*

And he wasn't even asking for himself. That's what drove Drew nuts. No, after a lifetime of selfishness, Frank was actually pulling a one-eighty. Doing something unselfish and asking for help for his son. His *other* son.

It wasn't Cole's fault. Drew didn't hate the kid. He felt

sorry for him—learning his dad was a deadbeat had clearly been a shock to Cole. As much of a shock as it had been for Drew to learn he had a half-brother.

In a funny way, Drew even felt a bit of admiration for the way Cole had stood up to him.

He's not a bad kid at all. He can't help the cards he's been dealt. Why not give him a hand? You can afford it.

College was expensive, but money wasn't the issue. Drew had plenty of cash. But it stuck in his craw to do Frank any favors, after all his lying and gameplaying.

You wouldn't be doing it for him. You'd be helping Cole. Why punish him for the old man's sins?

Frank must have taken Drew's silence for refusal, because his eyes narrowed and his expression turned cagey. "You asked me something the first time we talked. I laughed it off, but maybe I shouldn't have. You know, about going to the press. It might not be such a bad idea—I wonder how much the *National Weekly Scoop* or one of those other papers would pay for a story. 'Rich Retired Athlete Leaves Family in Poverty.' That would make a pretty juicy headline, don't you think? Sure would mess up that shiny image you keep polished. Me not going that route ought to be worth something to you."

Red hot fury pulsed behind Drew's eyes. He was almost frightened of how angry he felt. "Man, I knew you were low. But I didn't think even you could sink that deep."

Frank didn't flinch. Didn't back down. "Guess I'll do what I have to, to help my kid."

Drew balled his hands into fists to keep from grabbing the old man and shaking him. *No. Don't do it. This guy's not worth a minute of your time or a drop of your sweat. For sure not worth risking an assault charge. Don't engage.*

Just moments ago, he might have helped Cole, who seemed like a decent kid.

But now that Frank had threatened him? Drew wouldn't

play along. He wouldn't bow to anyone's blackmail. "Do what you gotta do, Frank. Go tell it all to the Snoop or some other rag. You're not getting a cent from me."

Time to get out of here before he completely lost his cool and gave Frank even more trash to report to the tabloids. "Don't contact me again. Ever."

He yanked the driver's door open so wide that Frank had to jump back to avoid getting smacked. Drew slid in behind the wheel, started the engine and peeled out of the lot.

As he drove home, it wasn't Frank who haunted him. It was Cole.

CHAPTER 18

Drew

Once home, Drew tugged off his street clothing, tossed his garments carelessly on the floor, then pulled on his running gear. Harley's ears perked up. He liked to go running, too.

"Sorry, guy. Another day." It wouldn't be fair to bring the dog along, because Drew meant to run himself into exhaustion. He had to punish himself. Punish himself for being fool enough to trust Frank. Being stupid enough to think the man might have ever cared about him.

He wanted to run until he couldn't think anymore. Which is what he did.

He came home panting and sluicing sweat. His shorts, t-shirt and underwear landed on the floor next to his other clothes as he peeled them off on his way to the shower. Then he stood under the shower head and let the steaming water pelt him until it ran cold.

But even that wasn't enough to clear his worries. Frank's threat was serious.

What happens now?

Drew didn't care what the supermarket rags said about him. But there were others to think of. His sister, Adrienne. She shouldn't have to endure this type of notoriety on top of the troubles in her marriage. And what about his parents? The last thing they needed was paparazzi crawling around, hounding them for photos and sound bites.

Sure, he could cave to Frank and pay him off. But even if he did, could the old man be trusted? He'd already proven himself to be a liar and a manipulator. He might easily take the money and still go to the tabloids. Or decide to circle back for more when the cash ran out. Once they got their claws in you, blackmailers never let you off the hook.

It was too big a risk. More than that, the thought of giving in to Frank's threats seemed cowardly and left a bad taste in Drew's mouth.

As he toweled off, another realization hit him with a sickening thud. Someone else who might be hurt by a scandal. Savannah. His relationship with her was only just beginning, but if the paps found out about it, would they go after her, too?

She was a teacher, for goodness sake. She'd worked hard for her profession and was justly proud of it. All the same, teachers were scrutinized not just by the principal and the school board, but by the entire freaking community. Any seeming misstep or notoriety could make her lose her job. What would that mean for her and Gracie?

He had to protect them. Couldn't let them get hurt.

His cell phone buzzed and when he glanced at the screen, a chill went through him. Savannah was calling, as though she knew he was thinking of her that very instant.

He picked up, his hands damp with sweat. "Yes. Hello."

"Hi, Drew." Her voice was soft. Tentative. "Gracie and I were just out doing a few errands and—"

He heard Gracie's voice exclaim "Ask him, Mom! Ask him."

"Shush, Gracie," Savannah murmured to her daughter. Addressing him, she went on. "Well, we're not far from your place and Gracie has something she made for you. So we wondered if we could stop by so she can give it to you."

"Uh…" Everything he was dealing with made him feel like his brain was stuck in neutral. "You want to come over here?"

"Just for a moment—"

"I want to say hi to Harley, too," Gracie exclaimed, again interrupting her mother.

Savannah's voice went down an octave. "It sounds like this isn't a good time—"

He wasn't up to seeing anyone but couldn't think of an excuse fast enough. "No, it's fine," he said quickly, speaking over her. "Come on by."

"We'll be there shortly. Thanks." Was it his imagination, or had her tone cooled?

True to her word, she and Gracie appeared on his front steps a few minutes later. Drew had thrown on a pair of sweatpants and an old tee shirt, his hair still damp when he opened the door. Harley had heard them drive up and was by his side, ready to greet them.

"I missed you," Gracie cried, wrapping her arms around Harley's neck while the dog swept his tongue across her cheek. "Look what I drew." She waved a paper in her hand. "Look. It's a picture of you and me. See? I'm Lightning Lass and you're Zap."

Harley snuffled it then looked at her as though he wasn't sure what he was supposed to do with it.

Savannah's smile was polite and stiff, reminding Drew of the first time they'd met. "Gracie, aren't you going to say hello to Mr. Woodson?"

"Oh. Yeah." Unruffled, Gracie released Harley and looked up at him. "Hi, Mr. Woodson. Want to see my picture?"

The little girl's smile made the knot in his gut loosen. "You bet I do. Let's see."

He admired the cute picture of a blond girl standing next to a black dog, both of them wearing red capes and shirts with lightning bolt insignias.

"You can keep it," she said. "Put it on your fridge door. That's what my mom does with all my pictures."

"Thank you." The sudden fullness in his throat embarrassed him. "That's exactly where I'll put it."

A silence followed, one that Gracie filled with more pats and hugs for Harley while the two adults sneaked awkward looks at each other.

Drew found his tongue. He couldn't just leave them standing on the doorstep. "Uh, come on in for a bit. Oh." His face grew hot as he noticed the trail of garments still littering the floor from hall to bath. "Hold on—" he bent and scooped up a sweat-dampened tee shirt.

Savannah eyed the things he'd shucked off and took a step back. "No. We...we've got to get home...we really shouldn't have come by on such short notice..."

"No, it's okay," he answered. But he knew his response was weak. The truth was, he really wished they would go. Their presence left him awash in guilt, knowing the mess he might be dragging them into.

She took her daughter's hand. "Come on, Gracie. Aunt Shelley's waiting for us."

"Aw..." the little girl gave Harley one last pat. "Bye, Harley." She skipped down the steps, then waved to Drew. "Bye. Don't forget about the picture, okay? Harley will like seeing it on the fridge."

"I'll remember. Thanks. I love it."

Gracie waved from the window as her mom pulled out of the driveway. Savannah didn't spare him so much as a look.

He felt sick. *Well, you messed that up but good.*

Maybe it was just as well. If Savannah thought he was a jerk, it might not trouble her when he put an end to their friendship.

To protect her and Gracie, he saw no other choice.

He closed the door and looked down at Harley, who gazed up at him with big brown eyes full of trust. Once again, guilt twisted Drew's gut.

"The question is, buddy, what on earth am I going to do about you?"

CHAPTER 19

Savannah

"I don't know what I was thinking," Savannah muttered, more to herself than to her sister, who sat next to her on their sofa. "I never should have gone over there."

"Well, tell me again what happened," Shelley said. "I don't see that you did anything wrong. What's got you so upset?"

"It's just…the way he acted. I could tell he didn't want us there."

"He didn't say that, did he?"

"Of course not. But he wasn't glad to see us. I was so embarrassed…I just got all cold. You know how I am sometimes."

Shelley nodded. "Uh-huh. The ice queen routine."

Savannah knew she could seem icy and remote when she was nervous or uncomfortable. But she *wasn't* a cold, uncaring person. The ice shield was just a way of protecting herself.

"I told him Gracie wanted to show him her picture. That was only part of the reason. The thing is, I wanted to see him too, but didn't have the nerve to say so." Cringing with embarrassment, she buried her face in her hands. "Oh, why did I do it? Why did I put so much importance on a little kiss?"

"Kiss?" Shelley yelped. "What kiss? You never said anything about that. What am I missing?"

Looking up at her sister, Savannah said "It was Halloween night. We'd just taken Gracie trick-or-treating and had a moment alone. We were talking and...it just happened. He kissed me. It hardly lasted a moment."

"Wait, wait. Hold up." Shelley wriggled closer, determined to ferret out every detail. "He kissed you. Like, on the cheek?"

"No. On the lips."

"On the—" Shelley gave a huff of exasperation. "I can't believe you! You never said a word about it. What's the idea, holding out on me like that?" Her eyes sparked with curiosity. "Okay. So. Deets. Was it good?"

"I told you, it was only a few seconds." Then, in response to Shelley's look of disapproval, she surrendered with a sigh. "It was amazing." A shiver passed through her just remembering it. His lips gently caressing her own...his body so close to hers...

"Yoohoo, Earth to Savannah."

Tugged back to the present, Savannah was faced with her sister's knowing smirk. "That good, huh?" Shelley bounced on the cushion with excitement, as though *she* was the one who'd been kissed. "So what happened then?"

"Nothing. I mean, it happened, then Gracie appeared and that was it. But it was one kiss. Just because I thought it was special doesn't mean *he* did. I'm sure it was just a spur of the moment thing. It meant nothing to him."

Shelley turned serious. "You don't know that."

"Shelley, please. He's a famous former athlete. He has his own television show. He's kissed dozens of women. I'm not conceited enough to think I'm special."

"You *are* special. Don't downplay yourself. You know he's gone out of his way to get close to you and Gracie. Taking in Harley. Spending time with you. My gosh, even going out trick or treating and taking the dog along. He didn't have to do any of that. Of course, he's interested in you."

With all her heart, Savannah wanted to believe that. But she'd made a fool of herself once before and wasn't about to make the same mistake twice. "Why'd he behave so strangely, then, when Gracie and I stopped by?" She felt so stupid where men were concerned, like a sixth-grader asking her friends *"Do you think he likes me? No, do you really think so?"*

"Well, maybe he was just out of sorts," Shelley answered. "Everyone's entitled to a bad day."

Savannah shook her head. "I don't know. I think it was more than that."

Shelley eyed her solemnly. "Drew's a good guy. When Ty was going through a bad time, Drew really stuck by him. Even when Ty was acting like a big fat jerk. Drew's not the kind of man to string a woman along."

Savannah wanted to believe that, but doubts wracked her.

"Well, we could sit here all day and speculate." Shelley's voice was tinged with impatience. "That won't fix anything. What you've got to do is spend some time alone with the man."

A flutter of panic passed through Savannah. "And do what?"

"Well...talk. Does he just want to be friends or is he interested in something more?"

Savannah rolled her eyes. "Oh, that's a perfect way to scare him off."

"You're not going to come right out and ask him, Van. You're going to...you know, be smooth. Get a sense of how he feels."

"Smooth," Savannah echoed doubtfully. Still, Shelley had

a point. Mooning over the man and driving herself crazy was no solution. She had to do *something*.

"Look, it's hard for adults to have a serious conversation with a six-year-old constantly around. So why don't I take Gracie out for dinner and a movie this Saturday and you invite Drew here?"

"You'd do that?"

Shelley grinned. "Sure. I'd love some bonding time with my niece. It'll be fun." She gave Savannah a shoulder bump. "And it'll give you a chance to get better acquainted with that hottie, Drew."

Shelley's enthusiasm was catching. Savannah began to relax and felt a tremulous excitement at the thought of being alone with Drew.

Don't get ahead of yourself, she told herself sternly. *Remember, you might be nothing more to him than a passing fancy.*

For years she'd hidden behind the wall she'd built to protect herself from ever being hurt again. But now the wall had cracked. And through that crack, Savannah could see a sliver of bright sunshine.

Was it safe to step into the sunlight? She hoped so.

CHAPTER 20

Savannah

She called Drew that same evening, before she lost her nerve, asking him by for coffee on Saturday afternoon. To her relief, he readily agreed.

Her heart stuttered when she caught sight of his car pulling up on Saturday. Wiping her damp palms on the fabric of her slacks, she told herself *Calm down. You're as jumpy as a schoolgirl meeting her first crush.*

Well, if she made a total fool of herself, only Drew would witness it. Shelley had taken Gracie out to a movie and an early dinner, as promised. Savannah stepped back from the window from which she'd been peering and forced herself not to rush to the door before hearing his knock. She wanted to seem casual. Not too eager.

Smooth, remember?

She was surprised when she opened the front door and saw that Drew had brought Harley with him. "Oh. Hello." She stood a moment, blinking in confusion before she remembered her manners. "Hi, come on in." She gave a small laugh. "I didn't quite expect you to bring our friend along." Harley grinned happily when she stroked his head. "Hi, fella."

"Yes, I...I want to explain," Drew answered, his brows lowering. He didn't look at all happy to see her, and his serious expression changed her nervousness to dread. He looked grim, like a man getting ready to deliver bad news. "I'm glad you called me, because I need to talk to you."

Her stomach clenched. "All right." None of this was unfolding the way she'd imagined—hoped—it might. "Well, let's not stand here at the door. Come in and sit down. I'll get the coffee ready. I made snacks, too. I hope you like—"

"I can't stay." He shifted his feet and grimaced. "I'm sorry. Something unexpected has come up and..." he let go a breath. "I'm leaving town."

"You—" she didn't know what to say. Her brain felt frozen and the ice had spread to her tongue.

"Yes." He looked from the floor to the ceiling to the wall just behind her left shoulder. "I know it's sudden but, uh, it can't be helped." When at last he gazed at her straight on, it was to offer her the dog's leash. "I'd like you to have Harley."

Still speechless, she gaped at him. He placed Harley's leash in her numb hand. "I can't bring him with me and I don't have the heart to take him back to the shelter. He loves Gracie and I know she feels the same way about him. He likes you a lot, too. He'll be happy here and I know you'll take good care of him."

Savannah couldn't think of anything beyond the fact that Drew was leaving town. *What's wrong with you? You knew from the start he didn't plan on staying. Did you really think a silly little kiss was going to change his mind? Did you really think you're that important to him?*

Taking advantage of her silence, Drew went on. "I know you've said you can't have him here. But hold on." He showed her the screen of his cell phone. "I've made all the arrangements. Set up monthly deliveries of dog food and some other necessities through this website here. It all comes right to your door. And at this site?" He opened a different tab. "I've set up an account so you can arrange for a dogwalker to take Harley out when you're at work or anytime you want. And I've spoken to the people at the Verona Lake Vet Clinic. You can take Harley there for his vaccinations and checkups, and they'll bill me. You won't have to worry about any of his expenses. I'll handle everything."

The ice surrounding her had cracked and Savannah could at last feel something. What she felt was pure anger.

"You're taking a lot for granted," she muttered. She glanced down at Harley, who stared up at her with innocent brown eyes. He had no idea that Drew, the man he trusted, was leaving him. Leaving them all.

And backing her into a nice little corner. Drew had thought of everything. Or just about.

As if he read her mind, he added "And you don't have to worry about your landlords. I've spoken to the Russos about how much Gracie loves Harley. They've got a real soft spot for your little girl. They've decided it's okay for Harley to stay with you. It didn't hurt that I sweetened the deal by promising them season tickets to all the Condors' games. Box seats." He smiled, as though hoping to win her over. "Did you know they're big baseball fans?"

She didn't respond to the question or the smile. Yes, he'd covered all the bases. And there was no way she could refuse without looking like—and feeling like—the world's biggest meanie.

It wasn't even that she *wanted* to refuse. She was fond of Harley and hated the thought of sending him back to the animal shelter, where he'd been so unhappy. She knew

Gracie would be thrilled to know he'd be living here with them. But Gracie had fallen not only for Harley, but for Drew as well. She'd miss him terribly.

So will I.

Savannah wanted to kick herself for being stupid enough to let her guard down. For letting herself catch feelings for this man who'd been careful never to make any promises. For letting him get close to her daughter.

She couldn't let Gracie lose Drew and Harley both. What choice did she have but to say yes?

"And Happy Hearts is all right with this?" she asked. "I thought the foster agreement said you had to return him to the shelter if you could no longer keep him."

"I've spoken to them. Though it's an unusual arrangement, they agreed to let me hand Harley over to you. They'll be doing the usual background check and home visit, but I don't think there'll be any problem with you keeping him."

She supposed he'd made a sizeable donation to persuade the shelter to bend its rules. *Money talks.*

"What about his things?" She kept her voice cool and under control. "I don't know, his food dishes, his bed? His toys. He needs those, too."

"I've got it all packed in the car," Drew answered. The tenseness in his features eased. "You mean you'll take him?"

"I don't see how I have much choice." This time she didn't bother to hide her bitterness. "Considering all the arrangements you've made. I can't let Harley go back to living in a cage. And I certainly can't let Gracie's heart get broken. I suppose it would sound petty of me to say I wished you'd consulted me before making all these plans."

He gave a small wince of guilt, and a mean little part of Savannah was glad. She knew he'd gone to a lot of trouble and was taking on considerable expense, smoothing Harley's transition from his house to hers. She ought to feel grateful.

Instead, she clung to her anger. It was all she had to protect her from the disappointment threatening to overwhelm her.

Drew went out to his car and carried in Harley's belongings and his bag of food. With his arms full, he said "Uh, where should I…"

"Just put it down right here," she said matter-of-factly, determined not to betray any more emotion. "I'll find a place for it all later."

"All right." He set the items down in the spot she indicated, then straightened. A muscle jumped in his jaw as he pinned her with a sad gaze. "Savannah, I—"

She spoke quickly to stop him from continuing. "You said you can't stay. Don't let me keep you."

She didn't want to hear what he might say. What could he say, anyway? That he was sorry?

If he was sorry, then why was he leaving?

His expression turned flat. "All right." Glancing from her to the dog, he gave Harley a lopsided smile and a pat on the head. "See you, guy. You be a good dog, now."

Harley panted, his tongue lolling. When Drew turned away and opened the door, Harley tugged at the leash, as though wanting to follow.

"No, Harley," Savannah murmured. "Stay."

Drew gave her one last look. "Goodbye."

Holding herself stiff and cold, avoiding his eyes, she answered. "Goodbye."

As soon as the door closed, she sagged. *It's over. Just be glad he didn't give you the chance to make a total fool of yourself.*

When she heard his car drive off, she looked down at Harley, who whimpered as if confused. His big brown eyes seemed to ask *"What's going on?"*

She squatted down to his level and fondled his ears. "It's okay, boy. We'll figure it out."

Who was she trying to convince? The dog or herself?

"We'll figure out how to get along without him."

CHAPTER 21

Drew

He drove aimlessly, stopping at random spots around town to kill a few hours before going home. When he got there, Drew tossed his keys onto a console table in the front hall and slunk into the living room feeling like the lowest form of life. A slug, maybe. Or not even that high up on the evolutionary ladder. Nah, he was lower than a slug. More like the slime trail a slug left behind.

Well, you messed that up but good, he told himself, thinking of how he'd left Savannah. *She really hates your guts now.*

Savannah thought he was a liar, a coward and a deadbeat who couldn't follow through with the commitment he'd made to Harley. And if he couldn't do that, then how could he possibly commit to a woman and child?

But what else could he have done? He couldn't tell her about Frank and the threats he'd made. Couldn't expose her and Gracie to all the sludge that the rags were sure to throw their way if the old man spilled his guts.

Of a bunch of lousy choices, he'd made the only choice possible.

Upon reaching the living room, he flopped into a leather armchair. His foot hit something and sent it rolling across the floor. One of Harley's tennis balls. Seeing it sent a pang through Drew's chest. Though Harley had only lived there a few weeks, the house already seemed too quiet and lonely without him.

He let out a sigh of surrender. His rotten day wasn't over yet. There were more unhappy tasks ahead of him. He could put them off a while, but they'd only loom larger the longer he waited.

No. He firmed his jaw and straightened his spine. *Do it now and get it over with.* He picked up his phone to video chat with Adrienne.

"Hey, sis," he said as soon as she appeared on screen.

Though he'd tried to sound jaunty, she picked up on his mood right away. "Hey, bruh. What's the matter?" Her carefully tended eyebrows descended as she looked at him in concern.

"Why'd you ask that?"

"Because you look like death warmed over, as the saying goes."

He rubbed his chin, feeling the bristles of his five o'clock shadow. Crud. If he looked as bad as he felt, he must be a mess.

"How are you and the girls?" He asked, knowing he was only delaying the inevitable with the conversational detour.

Adrienne was having none of it. "We're all right. But I want to hear about you." When he hesitated, she added "Come on. I've bent your ear often enough with my problems. It's only fair you let me share yours."

But it *wasn't* fair. Drew had always been proud of the fact that he was the big brother, looking out for his little sis. Watching out to make sure bullies didn't bother her and kids weren't mean. It had been his job to protect her—a job he'd gladly assigned himself.

When his mom and her dad first got married, Drew hadn't known quite what to make of Adrienne. To him, she'd been a pesky little kid who stared at him like he was from another planet.

That all changed when she'd run home from school one day in tears. She'd taken Miss Elly, her stuffed toy elephant, to school. Some big kids had gotten hold of it and kicked it around the playground. She'd rescued Miss Elly, but the toy was dirty and bedraggled, with stuffing coming out its middle.

Big fat tears had rolled from Adrienne's eyes as she'd held Miss Elly in her arms. "Now she's ruined! They killed her."

A hard lump formed in his chest when he saw her cry. "Naw, she's not dead," he'd told her. "Just a little messed up. You can give her a bath in the tub. Even use some of my mom's bubble stuff if you want."

Adrienne sniffled. "But all her insides are coming out."

"Lemme see." He took the toy and examined it the way he imagined a doctor might. Then he had an idea. "Just a minute."

He found a roll of duct tape and some scissors in a junk drawer. Carefully, he pushed the stuffing back inside Miss Elly. Then he wrapped a length of silver duct tape around its middle like a bandage covering a wound. He cut the end and patted it secure. "There." He handed the toy back to his new little sister. "She's good as new now. The bandage even kind of matches her fur. And it'll keep her butt from falling off."

He didn't know why he'd said that last part, but it made Adrienne giggle. That small giggle lit him up inside. Then she had looked up at him with big brown eyes full of admiration. Like he was her hero. When she'd slipped her hand into his, so trustingly, he made himself a promise. He would always try to be her hero.

And now, instead of protecting her, he was dragging her into his mess.

"It's not just my problem. That's the thing," he confessed.

Then he spilled his guts. Told her how Frank had contacted him. How he, Drew, in a mixture of curiosity and conceit, had let the man into his life. He told her about Cole, the brother he never knew existed. And about Frank's threats to go to the tabloids with his nasty spin on the whole story.

His sister's pretty face was somber, her eyes dark with sadness. "I'm so sorry. Finding your birth dad only to have him turn on you. You don't deserve that."

"If it was just me, I wouldn't care. But when this muck hits the rags, it's going to splatter you, too. And Mom and Dad. And Jordan."

Adrienne's full lips thinned at the mention of Jordan's name. "I doubt he'd even notice it. He doesn't notice much of anything lately that's not work related." Then she quickly shook her head. "Sorry. I didn't mean to derail."

"You and Jordan still not communicating?"

Adrienne scoffed. "It's a little hard to communicate with someone who's never home." She made a slashing motion with her hand. "Never mind that. I don't want you to worry about me. This Frank dude doesn't scare me. I'm just worried about what it's doing to *you*, Drew."

"Oh, I'm all right," he said dismissively.

"No. I don't buy that. Having your father come back into your life, only to—"

"He's not my father." The tightness in Drew's throat made his voice rough, rougher than he meant it to be. "Pop's the only father I've ever had. The only one I want."

"I know," Adrienne answered quietly. "And you're his son, in every way that counts. But you've got to be hurting, Drew.

You don't have to be so brave, you know. You've always tried to act like nothing bothers you. Like you've got it all together. But no one's got it all together all the time. You've always tried to shield us—me, Mom and Dad—from anything that might trouble you. Now don't deny it. I know it's true. Stop trying to protect us, Drew. We're family. Let us share your worries. We're strong enough to handle them."

The tightness in his throat intensified, making it impossible to speak, as tears stung his eyes. Humbled though he was by Adrienne's words, he wasn't surprised she'd seen through him. She was one smart cookie, his kid sister.

"It's not just you and the folks I'm worried about," he said when he managed to speak. "There are others that might be hurt, too. A woman I've come to know and her little girl."

"A woman?" Adrienne's eyes widened. "How serious is it?"

"There hasn't been enough time for things to get serious, but…"

His sister picked up the thread when his voice trailed off. "But you care about her. Who is she?"

"Her name's Savannah Kaminski. She teaches at the elementary school in town."

"And she has a daughter, you said?"

"Yeah. Gracie. A real cute little kid," he answered. A sharp pang hit him as he realized he might never see Gracie's sweet face again. "But you know how teachers get judged like crazy for things, things ordinary people do without a second thought. Like being seen in public having a beer. If Frank's story gets out, and people connect me with Savannah, it could blow up her career. I can't take the chance she'll get hurt."

"What does that mean?"

"It means I'm going to pack up and get the heck out of town. If the hounds follow me, at least I can lead them away from Savannah and Gracie."

"What does Savannah say to that?"

Drew shifted guiltily in his chair. "She doesn't know."

Adrienne jerked back her head in surprise. "What?"

"I mean, she knows I'm going, but I didn't tell her why—"

"*What?*" Her voice was so sharp it was nearly a shriek. "You didn't *tell* her?"

"I don't want her dragged into my mess. It's not fair."

"What's unfair is you not giving her the information she needs. Not allowing her to make her own decision. If you told her you're leaving and gave no explanation, she must think you don't care about her at all. That's how I'd feel in her shoes."

"I'm just trying to protect her."

"You're trying to play the hero and treating her like she's incapable of knowing what's right for her. I swear, you men. In your rush to 'protect' us you forget that we women are adults fully capable of standing on our own two feet. Just like Jordan—" Adrienne cut off her lecture and gave a huff of frustration. "No. I'm not going there. This isn't about me. It's about *you*—" She thrust her index finger forward as though she wanted to reach through the screen and poke him.

"I know she didn't see it coming," Drew admitted, awash in guilt. "She got real stiff, like I was a stranger. Acted like she couldn't wait to be rid of me, once I told her."

"She was probably hurting and didn't want you to see her break down. Been there."

"She did take Harley, though. At least I don't have to worry about him."

"Harley? The dog?" Adrienne's forehead creased in puzzlement. "What does he have to do with this?"

"Gracie's taken such a shine to him. Fallen head over heels for the crazy mutt. And he feels the same way about her. Once I'm back in the city I won't be able to give him the time he needs. And I didn't have the heart to take him back where he'd be in a cage all day. So—"

"So you guilted Savannah into taking him."

"No," he protested, though Adrienne wasn't far from wrong. "Nothing like that. I'll be paying for all his needs—food, vet care, whatever. And I cleared it with the landlord. She'll have no worries on that score."

"You presented her with a done deal and made it so she'd be the bad guy if she refused to take the dog. Not cool, bruh. I tell you what, I'm totally Team Savannah on this."

"Ugh." He groaned, scrubbing his face with the palm of his hand. "I didn't mean to make such a mess of it."

Adrienne eyed him pityingly. "I guess not. Still, you did a bang-up job. What happens now?"

"Now I call Mom and Pop and warn them about Frank." Confession was supposed to be good for the soul, right? Then why did he feel so exhausted? So empty? "I don't want them to be surprised by any nosy paps showing up on their doorstep."

"You look beat." Adrienne's face softened with sympathy. "Why don't you just get some sleep and take care of the rest tomorrow?"

There was nothing he'd like more. "I might just do that. I haven't heard any more from Frank, so another day might not make a difference."

"I'm sure it won't. Get some rest. And keep me in the loop, for heaven's sake. Bye, Drew. Love you."

"Love you too." He ended the call. Then he stood and headed to his bedroom. He'd call the folks first thing in the morning. Tonight he'd get into bed, pull the covers over his head, and let the sandman dissolve his worries.

CHAPTER 22

Harley

I live with Gracie, Mom and Aunt Shelley now. Gracie was so surprised and happy when she found me here. She clapped her hands and let out a squeal as if somebody stepped on her tail. But it was a happy squeal, and she doesn't have a tail. I am very happy because I love Gracie.

But I am sad too because I miss my friend Drew. Will I ever see him again? I thought he liked me, but then he left me here. Why did he do that? I tried very hard to be Good. I even stopped playing the Smelly game when I found out he didn't like it.

I wish I understood the secret to being a Good Dog.

It is strange to feel happy and sad at the same time. But I don't think about it too much when I am with Gracie. We play lots of good games. Sometimes we play Lightning Lass and Zap and we rescue her Teddy Bear from bad guys. Sometimes she is a fairy princess and I am the dragon who protects her. When her friend Randi comes over, we play dolls then go outside and play Catch the Ball.

I am allowed to sleep in Gracie's room, on the floor next

to her bed. But when Mom tells us good night and turns off the light, Gracie pats the bed and I creep up very quietly to snuggle beside her. She says I am her protector and give her sweet dreams. That makes my heart feel big and warm and happy. I am proud to help my Gracie. She is my best friend.

But I think Gracie misses Drew, too.

"Did Mr. Woodson really give us Harley for keeps?" She asks Mom tonight at supper. We eat supper together in the kitchen. While my people eat supper at the table, I eat my yummy kibble from my special dish on the floor.

"Yes," Mom says.

"But why? Doesn't he want Harley anymore?"

"He's leaving town, dear. And he...well, he can't take Harley with him. So he gave him to us."

"He's going away?" Gracie's eyes look big and hurt. I whimper. I do not want my friend to feel sad. "But I thought he liked it here. I thought he liked us."

Mom's mouth goes flat. "He...likes us. Of course, he does. But he has his own life. He never meant to stay in Verona Lake for long."

"But he's gonna come back, isn't he?"

Mom whooshes out a long breath like she is tired. "Gracie, I don't know what the man plans to do. Why all the questions? I thought you wanted Harley here."

"I do. But Mr. Woodson should come say goodbye to us and Harley. Isn't he going to do that?"

"Gracie, stop questioning me and finish your meal. It's getting cold." Mom rubs her forehead with her hand as though her head hurts.

"Why are you getting mad?" Gracie asks.

"I'm not mad. I just want you to finish eating."

But I think Mom is saying a fib. She *is* mad. And sad. People don't always say the truth about their feelings, but us dogs know what is really going on. We are smart that way.

I give a little whine because I do not want any of my people to be sad. It makes me sad, too. I leave the rest of my kibbles in the bowl and trot over to Mom and stand next to her chair so she can pet me. Maybe that will make her happy. But she doesn't look at me, so I nudge her arm with my nose. *Hello. Here I am! I am your friend and I like you.*

She frowns at me. "Harley, no. Get away from the table. Go eat your food."

Doesn't she know she should pet me? I nudge her arm again.

"No!" She raps the tabletop with her knuckles and makes a loud noise that hurts my ears. I yip and run to my corner.

Gracie's mouth turns down and her eyes get pinchy. "Don't yell at Harley."

"He needs to learn to stay away from the table while we eat. He mustn't start begging for table scraps. They're bad for him."

"Well, you don't have to yell. That's mean."

"I don't need any more of your remarks, young lady. Finish your dinner."

Gracie pokes out her chin. "I don't want any more. It's yucky."

I think Gracie is saying a fib because her dinner smells yummy to me. I would be happy to eat it, but Mom doesn't let me have people food.

Now Mom's eyes get all pinchy. "That's very rude."

Gracie's chin pokes out even further. "I don't care."

Oh no. What is happening? My people are being mad at each other. Worry twists in my chest. *No, no, family. Do not be mad. We love each other and must be Good.*

"Then you can leave the table and go right to your room," Mom says.

"Okay." Gracie climbs off her chair and calls me. "Come on, Harley."

My hungry tummy wants to finish the kibbles left in my dish, but Gracie is more important than food. She needs me so I follow her.

"Mean old grouch," she mutters on her way out of the kitchen.

"I heard that, young lady," Mom snaps in an angry voice.

Gracie slams her bedroom door loud, which makes my ears stand up and my fur prickle. She never closes the door. Even when it's bedtime she leaves it open a crack. She sits on the bed wearing a grumpy face. My smart ears can hear the words she whispers under her breath. They are mean and angry words.

Then she gets off the bed and digs out her box of crayons from her toybox in the corner. She gets the pad of paper she draws pictures on and climbs back on the bed. Lying there on her tummy, she draws a round face with a big open mouth and lots of sharp teeth. Two little black eyes and yellow hair that sticks straight out. Then she picks out another crayon and colors in the face. She presses so hard on the crayon that it snaps in two, but she doesn't stop coloring until the drawing is finished. Then she shows it to me. "There. See?"

I see. But who has a mean face like that?

With a new crayon she writes some words on the paper. "Mom...is... a..." she stops and taps the crayon to her chin. "Hmm...m...e...e...n..." she writes it down then slides off the bed and opens the door.

She calls down the hall. "Mom?"

"What is it?" Mom calls back.

"How do you spell grouch?"

"G...r...o..." Mom comes into the hall and looks at her. "What are you doing?"

"Never mind." Gracie shuts the door again and finishes writing. "G...r...o..." she stops to think then adds "Chuh."

She holds the paper out to me again and reads "Mom is a mean grouch. Ha." Her mouth curves up but it is not a happy smile. She knows her picture is not nice. Mom does not look like that. She does not have a big round head with sharp teeth. But Gracie doesn't care. She is mad and sad just like Mom.

I stay with Gracie in her bedroom while she draws more pictures and reads some of her books. Later I hear Aunt Shelley come home. She and Mom talk in low voices in the living room. When I paw at the door Gracie opens it for me and I pad down the hall into the kitchen. Maybe I can finish the rest of my supper now.

I am oh so sad when I see that Mom took my dish away and my yummy kibbles are all gone. I am even sadder when my ears hear how Mom and Aunt Shelley are talking to each other.

"There's no need for you to take your bad mood out on me," Aunt Shelley says. "You've been like this ever since Drew told you he's leaving town."

"That's got nothing to do with it," Mom answers, her voice snappish. "And if you're not happy being here, you can leave any time you like."

Aunt Shelley is quiet for a minute. "Is that what you want me to do?" Her voice is soft.

"I didn't say that." Mom's voice is soft too. "But I'm certainly not forcing you to stay."

Oh no. My people are not happy and they are saying things to hurt each other's feelings. I whimper. *Please stop it, family. Please be Good to each other.*

I must help my family. It is my job to cheer them up. Then we can all be happy and love each other. I get an idea when I see the kitchen towel hanging from the handle of the fridge door. I pull it out with my teeth and trot into the living room with it in my mouth. We can play a fun game of Chase Me and no one will be mad anymore.

I go up to Mom who is sitting beside Aunt Shelley on the sofa. She frowns when she sees me holding the towel and tries to pull it away but ha ha I am too smart and fast. I bounce away from her and wag my tail. *Come chase me! We will have fun and be happy!*

Still frowning, she turns away. Why won't she chase me?

Maybe Aunt Shelley will play. I go around the coffee table and nudge her arm with my nose. *Hello! I am so funny here with this towel. Come chase me and we will play!*

"Just ignore him," Mom says. "He'll get tired of it and leave us alone."

No, no. I cannot leave them alone. I must help us all be happy again. I nudge Aunt Shelley once more and my waggy tail makes a mistake and knocks over a glass on the coffee table.

I whimper as water runs off the table onto the floor. I did not mean for that to happen. Aunt Shelley quickly tugs the towel from my mouth and mops up the spill.

"Give me that," Mom says, taking the wet towel and the glass. Then she glares at me. "Bad boy."

My ears droop sadly and so does my tail. My heart feels sore and squooshy inside me. I am a Bad Boy. Even when I try to help my family, I am Bad.

Slowly I go back to Gracie's room and lie on the floor next to her bed. She has her pjs on and pats the bed for me to get up beside her. But turn my head away because I am too ashamed. I am too Bad to snuggle next to my Gracie.

When Mom comes in to say goodnight, Gracie pretends she is already asleep. Mom looks at me with sad eyes and I hide my head in shame. She turns off the light and leaves the door open a crack like always.

I cannot sleep because I am too worried about my family.

Everyone is unhappy and saying mean, angry things to each other. I get in trouble when I try to help. My heart is as sad as an empty food dish.

I give an unhappy sigh. I don't think I will ever understand the secret to being Good.

CHAPTER 23

Drew

A week after he'd left Harley with Savannah, Drew was surprised by someone ringing his doorbell well after midnight. The incessant ringing jerked him out of the doze he'd fallen into watching some infomercial in the TV room. Dragging himself from the recliner, he staggered down the hall, wondering who'd be bothering people at this ungodly hour. After peering through the peephole, he immediately opened the door and gaped at the tall Black man illuminated by the exterior light.

"Well, can I come in?" His stepfather, Henry Woodson, asked. "Or you gonna leave me standing on the doorstep in the dark?"

Drew blinked, stepping back to let his Pop enter. "Uh, sure. Come on in." As the older man stepped past him, Drew peered out the door. "Where's Mom? She's not with you?"

Pop shook his head. "Oh, she wanted to come. I had a whale of a time convincing her not to. I figured we needed some time alone for a little man-to-man talk, just you and I."

He set down the small travel bag he'd brought with him. "Don't tell me you're too grown now to hug your old man?"

Though still confused, Drew gratefully embraced the only man who'd ever been a father to him. The man who'd stepped up to raise a brash, scared kid. Who had adopted that kid, given him love and his last name. Just knowing he was there eased Drew's troubled mind. Henry might have gained a little weight and gotten a bit grayer over the years, but he was still the rock that Drew, his mom, and his sister Adrienne had always leaned on.

"Your mom and I have been talking ever since we got your call," Henry told him when the hug ended. "Been talking to Adrienne, too. She's worried about you."

"She shouldn't be. Neither should you. I'm all right. Why didn't you call me, let me know you were coming?"

"Cause I wasn't in the mood for your phony excuses why I shouldn't come."

"I could've at least picked you up. What'd you do, the last plane to get here?"

"Flight was delayed. Was sitting in the airport for five hours waiting for them to give the go ahead. And I'm in better shape than you," Pop answered.

Drew rubbed his stubbled chin in embarrassment and ran a hand through his unkempt hair. He hadn't been sleeping well and the lack of rest was dragging him down. Though he'd planned at getting out of town as soon as possible, the arrangements were taking more time than he'd anticipated.

And truth be told, even though he knew it was the right decision, he didn't want to go. He missed Savannah and Gracie. He missed Harley.

"Your mother and I are disappointed it took you so long to tell us about Frank turning up," Pop went on.

Drew's cheeks grew hot. "I didn't want you to worry. But

now that he's threatened to stir up trouble, I had no choice but to tell you. You need to be prepared, just in case…"

Pop shook his head and tsked. "Boy, don't you know us by now? Your mother and I can handle ourselves just fine. No need to worry about us. A little gossip's not going to hurt us."

Yeah, he should have figured Henry and his mom were made of tougher stuff. After all, they'd faced gossip before, navigating an interracial marriage in the small, none-too-progressive town in which he'd grown up.

He thought back to the first time he met Henry and Adrienne. He'd been a kid and his mom surprised him one night by suggesting they go for ice cream after supper. That was unusual. There wasn't a lot of extra money for special treats, but since she proposed it, he'd readily agreed.

Even more surprising was the way Mom had fixed herself up for the outing—she'd changed into a nice dress, poofed up her hair, put on lipstick and even some perfume. She acted kind of giddy and lighthearted on the drive to the Dairy Princess. There was a sparkle in her eyes and a flush on her cheeks which made Drew suspicious, but the prospect of a double-decker chocolate cone helped him ignore his doubts.

As soon as they reached the Dairy Princess his mom scanned the cluster of people gathered outside. She gave a girlish titter when she spotted the Black guy sitting on a bench, a little girl in braids seated next to him.

"Oh, look. It's that nice Mr. Woodson who comes by the diner every day." His mom worked breakfast and lunch shifts at Pickler's Diner. "And that must be his daughter with him. What a nice surprise. Let's go over and say hello. Come on, now."

It was the last thing Drew wanted to do, but the sooner he got it over with, the sooner the double-decker cone would be his. He wanted to roll his eyes while his mom and the tall guy went on about what a coincidence for them to meet at the Dairy Princess and wasn't it such a funny surprise.

Yeah, right, Drew wanted to say. By then he'd figured out it was all a set-up. His mom and this guy had arranged to meet here. She *liked* him. Drew could tell by the way her cheeks got all rosy when she looked at the guy, and how her voice got high and fluttery when she talked to him.

Drew didn't like this at all. Who was this Woodson dude, anyway? Mom didn't need him. She had Drew. He looked out for her just like she looked out for him. They didn't need anyone else.

The little Kindergarten kid Mr. Woodson brought along didn't look happy about the situation, either. She clung to her father's hand like she was scared he might desert her. Her big eyes flashed from her dad to Drew, as though she didn't know what to make of him.

"I thought we were gonna get ice cream." Drew spoke loudly, interrupting the adults' conversation.

His mother gave him a tight-lipped glare that meant *Watch your manners.*

Mr. Woodson just laughed and said "That's right. We won't get it standing out here talking, will we? Let's get in line. Adrienne, what flavor do you want, baby girl? What about you, Drew?"

The man went up to the window, ordered and paid for all their ice creams. They returned to the bench and together sat eating their treats. Somehow Drew's mom ended up sitting on one end of the bench next to Mr. Woodson while Drew sat on the other end. Between him and her father was little Adrienne, who stared up at Drew while her strawberry cone melted, sending pink rivulets down her small brown hand.

Ten-year-old Drew frowned at the Kindergarten baby. "You're making a mess."

Mr. Woodson turned and mopped up Adrienne's hand

with a fistful of napkins. "Baby, eat your ice cream. Don't just let it melt."

The girl obediently took a lick of her cone while her dad and Drew's mom went back to their conversation. Drew's lip curled as his mom giggled at something the man said, while the Woodson guy laughed softly.

He felt Adrienne watching him and when he glanced her way, their eyes met. From the look on her face, he figured they were both thinking the same thing: *"What do these crazy grownups think they're doing?"*

"You got a coffee maker?" Pop asked, bringing Drew back to the present. "I sure could use a cup."

"Sure. Come on." He led Pop into the kitchen where he brewed a cup for each of them. As they sat, he said "You didn't need to come up here. Like I told you, I'm fine."

"I know that's what you say. That's what you've always said, even when you were a boy. You were always looking out for your mother, trying to protect her. For a while there, you wanted to protect her from me, too." Pop grinned and shook his head. "You sure gave me a hard time when you found out I wanted to marry her."

The truth was, Drew had resented the new man in his mother's life, when it had always been just the two of them. But he felt bad, too, because he knew Henry Woodson made his mom happy. And he wanted her to be happy. Drew had been miserable, torn between jealousy and guilt.

One evening while he sat on the porch steps, watching Boomer play in the backyard, his mom had slipped beside him. Sliding her arm around his shoulder, she'd told him "It's just been you and me for a long time, hasn't it, son? I know I used to say that you were the man of the house, but now I think that was wrong of me. It was too much to put on your shoulders. You're still a boy, and it's not your job to take care of me. It never was. Henry is a good man. He's been raising his little girl on his own since his wife passed away. He wants us all to be a family—you and me and him and Adrienne. I want that, too. So, I'd like you to give him a chance. Promise me you'll try."

Unable to speak for the huge knot in his throat, Drew had nodded. Blinking back tears, he buried his face in his mother's shoulder. He couldn't tell her the truth—that he was scared of losing her. But he wanted her to be happy, so he would try, for her sake.

It hadn't been easy, for him or Henry. But little by little they came to trust and love each other.

"You didn't give up on me, though," Drew answered.

"I saw how much you loved your mom. How much you wanted to protect her. And how scared you were, under that tough act you put on."

Drew's face went hot and his throat tightened. He was grateful Pop had seen through him. Had seen the kid who'd been abandoned by his birth father, who toughed it out, pretending that it didn't matter. But deep down, Drew had always wondered if it was his fault that Frank had split, leaving him and his mom alone.

"You're still doing it, too," Henry went on. "Acting tough. Like it doesn't trouble you. But you can't tell me it doesn't hurt, having this Frank appear in your life after all these years, only to ask for money. And threaten to go to the papers if you don't hand it over."

"He's a stranger," Drew said. "I don't even know him. I don't care what he does, as long as he leaves my family alone." A pang shot through him as he thought of Cole. *He* was family, too. And a stranger. A brother he would never get to know.

"Yep. There you go again. Pretending it doesn't matter," Pop said.

Drew was losing patience. "What do you want me to do?"

he snapped, his voice rough with frustration. "Bust out crying? I'm not wasting any tears on Frank Flanagan."

"I want you to have a little faith in us. The people who love you. Stop trying to protect us. We're strong enough to handle whatever trouble this Flanagan brings. And we're strong enough to support you. We're family. We've got your back."

Pop gazed at him with deep compassion. "Your whole life, you've pushed yourself. Wanting to succeed, to make us proud. To make yourself proud. But I think something else was driving you, too. I think some part of you wanted to prove something to the man who abandoned you. Show him how wrong he was to leave you, even if he wasn't around to see it. Well, let me tell you something. You have nothing to prove. You never did."

Drew sat unmoving, feeling as though a boulder had just flattened him. His thoughts flew to his first meeting with Frank. What he'd wanted to say then: *"I've got more money than you'll see in a lifetime. Ten lifetimes. None of it thanks to you. You walked out like I was nothing. Well, I'm not nothing anymore, friend. How d'you like me now?"*

Pop stood, giving a tired sigh. "I hope that silence means you're thinking over what I've said. In the meantime, you need to show me a bedroom, 'cause I'm beat. I've got to call your mother, let her know I'm here, then get some sleep. We can talk more come morning."

"Sure." The word came out a croak from Drew's thick, froggy throat.

After settling Pop in a guest room, he stumbled into his own room and flopped onto the bed.

Was his Pop right? Had Drew really spent his life pursuing success, trying to excel, so he could prove something to the deadbeat who'd left him and his mom alone?

It was a heck of a lot to think about.

CHAPTER 24

Harley

Gracie is asleep in her bed, but I am wide awake. I am too worried about my family to sleep. I circle and lie down, stand up and circle again. Nothing feels cozy and comfortable. My fur feels itchy and my nose is twitchy and I cannot settle down. Something feels wrong, but I do not know what it is.

At last my eyes close. When they open again, the house is very dark and quiet. My fur stands on end and I jump to my paws. Something Bad is happening! Something is sneaking into the house to hurt my family! A dark cloud is hovering over our heads trying to hurt us! It smells Bad, stinging my eyes and nose and hurting my throat.

I bark at it. *Go away, Bad Thing! Leave my family alone!*

It is not going away. It wants to come down to hurt my Gracie!

I jump onto the bed, barking and whimpering. I lick Gracie's face to wake her up. We must get away from this Bad Smelly cloud!

Gracie moans and stirs, then sits up and coughs. Then she screams. "Mommeee!"

Yes, Gracie! We must get Mom and run away from the Bad Thing!

I stick my nose into the door crack and open it all the way, then race into the living room. I jump on the sofa where Aunt Shelley is sleeping and I woof and woof. I throw myself against Mom's closed door and bark as loud as I can. A moment later, Mom flings the door open, coughing and crying Gracie's name.

Yes, Mom! Let's get Gracie and all run away!

We run to Gracie's room. She is on the floor crawling toward the door. Mom tries to pick her up but Gracie tells her "Get Low and Go, Mommy!"

I am already low. My people crawl on their hands and knees to the front door, calling each other's names to make sure we are all together. I go with them and keep near Gracie. *Don't be afraid, my Gracie, I will never leave you alone with this Bad Thing.*

Mom touches the door to make sure it isn't hot. When she knows it is safe to open, we tumble down the stairs and out to the street. Aunt Shelley pounds at the Russo's door to wake them up while Mom, Gracie and I run to a neighbor's house to have them call 911.

Soon we are all waiting on the neighbor's porch watching the big trucks drive up. They flash bright lights and make loud Woo Woo sounds that hurt my ears. While the people talk about "smoke" and "fire," I tremble. When my Gracie kneels next to me and strokes me, I feel better. She is smart and brave, to Get Low and Go.

"You saved us, Harley," she whispers in my ear. "You're a hero, just like Zap."

My heart feels big in my chest and as happy as a food bowl full of kibble and a box of brand-new squeaky toys. Gracie is proud of me.

I am proud of me, too.

CHAPTER 25

Drew

The next morning, while Pop was sleeping in, Drew's phone dinged. Someone had messaged him.

This is Cole. Can I talk to you?

Drew went cold. He stared at the screen, tempted to ignore the request. A few moments later, he typed *What is it?*

I'd like to see you in person. Can we meet somewhere?

What was this about? Was it some trick? *I don't want to see your father*, he responded, momentarily forgetting that he and Cole had the same father.

He's already gone. It's just me.

What did the kid want? Drew didn't owe him anything. Then he remembered that none of this was Cole's fault. He'd been just as blindsided by Frank's secrets as Drew had been. They had that much in common, anyway.

That, and blood.

Lakeview Diner is just down the street from the motel. Meet me there.

OK. When?

Drew hesitated, then steeled himself. No reason to put it off.

Now.

* * *

The kid was sitting at a booth in the diner, facing the door. His eyes met Drew's the moment Drew entered. Drew nodded at the server behind the front counter and took a seat across from Cole.

Cole looked nervous, his face pale except for two red blotches on his cheeks. His Adam's Apple bobbed jerkily as he took a sip from his cup of coffee. "Hey."

"Hey yourself," Drew answered, still wary.

A smiling server popped up beside him. "Hi. Can I take your order?"

"Yeah. Coffee, please. Black. And, uh, a cheese omelet. With bacon. And whole wheat toast." He wasn't hungry but didn't want to take up the booth without ordering anything. And stuffing his face would give him something to do while he listened to whatever Cole had to say.

"Of course. Would you like home fries with that?"

"Sure," he answered. "Thank you." He glanced at Cole. "Uh, you want anything? Some eggs? Pancakes or something?" Then, thinking the kid might be short on cash, Drew added "It's on me."

The kid jerked up his head, anger sparking in his eyes. "No."

When the waitress left, Cole muttered "I don't need your money."

So he'd offended the kid with his offer. "Take it easy. Don't get so worked up."

"No. I mean I don't want your money. Any of it. My dad told me what he said to you. How he'd trash you if you didn't give me college money. I told him I'm not gonna be any part of a dirty scheme like that. Told him if he went ahead with it, I'd stop talking to him. Cut him out of my life."

Drew fell momentarily silent. The kid had guts. "What did Frank say?"

"He was like, shocked. I don't know why. He and Mom raised me better than that. They taught me morals. What he's talking about, it's like, blackmail. Right?" Cole shook his head. "I'm not about that."

Drew couldn't wrap his head around Frank knowing anything about morals, much less teaching them. But it was different for Cole. "Do you want to go to school?"

"Yeah, sure. But not that way. I'll figure it out. Other people do. Loans. Working my way through. I'm not good enough at sports to get a scholarship, but I'll manage."

This kid was tough and smart. Drew had no doubt he'd manage, though his road would be longer and harder.

"Anyway…I just wanted to let you know you don't have to worry about Dad going to the press or whatever. He's not gonna mess up your life. He wasn't thinking right when he threatened you. He just wanted to help me, you know? When I told him off, I think he was ashamed of himself." Cole's cheeks puffed as he released a long breath. "So, that's why I wanted to see you. To tell you face to face that I wasn't any part of this."

"I never thought you were."

Drew gazed at his half-brother with growing respect. Refusing to fall in line with Frank's threats took courage. So did coming here to face Drew man to man.

I could help him. Not because of anything to do with Frank, but because Cole was a decent guy who deserved a chance at a better life.

Even as Drew turned the thought over in his mind, he

decided not to mention it. He sensed the kid might view it as "charity" and not take well to it.

When the waitress returned with his order and set it on the table, Drew noticed Cole eyeing it hungrily. Pushing the plate over to the younger man, Drew told the waitress "Another one, just the same, please?"

Cole hesitated a moment, but the mouth-watering aromas of bacon and seasoned home fries were too much for him. He forked off a big bite of the cheesy omelet and jammed it into his mouth, rolling his eyes rapturously as he chewed.

Drew stifled a grin. "Tell me more about you."

* * *

They ate, conversing throughout the meal. Cole did most of the talking and Drew was happy to listen.

As he listened, his respect for Cole only grew. They had more in common than sharing a birth father. Frank might have been a better dad to Cole than he'd been to Drew, but he was far from perfect. For a long time he had trouble keeping jobs and the family struggled. When Frank finally got into over-the-road trucking, his job often kept him far from home. Cole was close to his mother and saw himself as her protector. From the time he was a kid, he'd had jobs to help bring in money—paper routes, yard work for neighbors, running errands.

Strangely, there was no bitterness in Cole's voice as he told his story. He still loved Frank, in spite of the man's shortcomings.

Even stranger, Drew felt no resentment or bitterness. Frank might have cleaned up his act for Cole, but Drew was the luckier man. Because he'd had a *real* father in Pop.

By the end of their meal, Cole trusted Drew enough for

them to exchange phone numbers. Cole promised he'd keep in touch. And Drew had made up his mind to do whatever he could to help his brother attain his dream of going to college.

Just as he slipped behind the wheel of his car, his phone binged. It was a text from Ty.

Have you seen this?

The message included a link, which opened to the video of a local newscast.

He watched in shock as young female reporter spoke to the camera outside Savannah and Gracie's home.

"This is Belinda Casey coming to you from the town of Verona Lake. What might have been a tragic story has turned into a tale of heroism and devotion. Early this morning a fire broke out at 428 Ashwood Ave. Two families were fast asleep and might not have awakened in time if not for the courage of a newly adopted pet."

There was a cutaway to the Chief of the local fire department who mentioned the cause of the fire as faulty electrical wiring. "There was considerable smoke which should have set off the building's smoke alarms, but apparently the batteries had not been checked in quite a while. The people inside were very fortunate to have escaped."

"That's an important lesson for all of us, to make sure our smoke alarms are in working condition," the reporter said. "Thank you, Chief."

The camera pulled back from the reporter's face to reveal Savannah and Gracie standing next to her and with them, Harley.

"I'm here with two people who were inside when the fire broke out—Savannah Kaminski and her daughter Gracie. Also here is their dog, Harley. His barking sounded the alarm to wake his family and get them all safely outside. The other occupants of this two-family home, Mr. and Mrs. Albert Russo, also escaped safely."

The reporter turned to Savannah. "That must have been a terrifying experience, Ms. Kaminski. Thank goodness Harley was there."

"Yes." Savannah looked pale, as though still shaken by the experience. Who could blame her? But when she glanced at Harley, her eyes shone with love. "I'm very grateful. And so glad he's part of our family."

Ms. Casey replied "And what do you say, Gracie?"

"Harley's the best dog in the whole world," Gracie answered. "I love him to infinity."

"And I'll be he feels the same way about you."

Harley gave a loud woof of agreement, making Gracie giggle and the grownups smile. "You heard it from the hero himself, viewers. This is Belinda Casey for WSPR News."

The clip ended. Drew sat staring at the screen of his phone. It took him a moment to realize that his eyes ached and his cheeks were wet. He was crying.

With the heel of his hand, he wiped away the tears. Tears of pride for Harley's courage were mixed with those of relief and gratitude, when he considered what might have happened to Savannah and Gracie had the dog not been there.

They might have died.

They might have died, never having wakened.

The chief said it had been an electrical fire with a lot of smoke. Was the house too damaged for them to return? Drew knew the Red Cross often found hotel rooms for displaced families.

He texted Ty. *Where are they now?*

At my place. Staying here until it's okay to go back.

Drew texted back. *I'll be right over.*

CHAPTER 26

Drew

He'd left Pop a note before going to meet Cole. Unsure when he'd be back home, Drew sent him a quick text.

Got one more stop to make. Help yourself to whatever's in the fridge.

Some host. You got nothing in there but beer and some moldy fruit. Where in blazes are you? Pop shot back.

I'll explain later. Drew replied. *Order a pizza to go with the beer. I'll pay for it.*

You bet you will. Okay, see you later, man of mystery.

At Ty's place, he rang the bell and his friend let him in. Seeing the look on Drew's face, Ty wasted no time on greetings. "They're in back."

In the back yard, Savannah and Gracie were playing with Harley while Shelley looked on. Ty's fuzzy Persian cat was curled on her lap. Shelley waved him over.

"How are you?" He peered at her intently, his heart racing. The question was more than a mere pleasantry.

She gave him a small smile. "All right. It was scary, but…"

As her voice trailed away, he glanced meaningfully at Gracie and her mother. "And…?"

"You should ask them yourself."

At that moment Gracie spotted him and raced over to him. Harley trailed her with a joyful woof. "Mr. Woodson! Hi!"

"Hi, Gracie." His mouth stretched into a smile even as his eyes again grew wet. Hoping the little girl wouldn't notice, he playfully scrubbed the top of Harley's head. "Hey, guy."

Gracie and the dog crowded him, vying for his attention. "Did you see us on TV? There was a bad fire, but Harley woke us up and saved us! And I remembered to 'Get Low and Go' just like the firefighters taught us in school."

"I saw you, yes." He blinked rapidly as his vision swam and Gracie's little face went blurry. His throat felt thick and tight when he spoke. "I'm so proud you remembered. A lot of people forget the rules when there's a fire. Even grown-ups. You were really brave."

Gracie beamed, standing taller. "Harley was brave, too. He's a hero. The firefighters said. And he's gonna get a medal, too!" Her smile faded and her forehead creased as she gazed at Drew in puzzlement. "Mr. Woodson? Are you crying?"

Yes. Yes, he was. He turned away as he wiped his cheeks, not wanting to upset the child. "It's okay, Gracie. Don't mind me."

"Mom?" Gracie called, confusion and a bit of fear in her voice.

Savannah, who until then had stood back, quickly stepped to her daughter's side. "It's all right, sweetie."

"But he's—"

"We've talked about this, right? Sometimes our feelings get too big inside and we need to let them out. Tears help us do that."

"But they're for being sad," Gracie said, as though still confused.

"Not always," Savannah answered.

"That's right." Drew turned back toward them, embarrassed by his show of emotion, yet not regretting it. "These aren't sad tears, honey. They're happy ones. I'm so happy you and your mom and Aunt Shelley weren't hurt in the fire. That you're all safe and sound."

"Harley, too," Gracie said. "Don't forget him."

"Of course not." He glanced at the dog, who sat watching him expectantly. "How could I forget Harley?"

Gracie peered at him, her eyes narrowing. "Mom said you're moving away. Did you come to say goodbye? Is that why you're here?"

He shook his head. "No." Though he hadn't realized it until this moment, he knew he wasn't going to leave Verona Lake. Not as long as Savannah and Gracie were here. "I came to see you. My plans have changed. I'm not going anywhere."

He heard Savannah's sharp intake of breath before Gracie whooped. "Yay! I'm glad. I bet Harley is, too." Then her expression grew worried. "We can still keep him, can't we? You're not going to take him back?"

"No, honey." He addressed Gracie but gazed only at Savannah when he spoke. "He's yours for keeps."

CHAPTER 27

Savannah

"Hurray!" Gracie gave the dog a hug while Drew stayed caught in Savannah's gaze.

Shelley cleared her throat and stood, dislodging the big gray cat who went to sit in the shadow of a large bush. "Gracie, why don't you come with me for a minute? Ty's been in the house a while. Let's go see what he's up to."

"Okay." Gracie followed her aunt into the house.

Savannah remained silent until the door closed behind them. The neckline of her sweater suddenly felt too tight, its weave itchy on her too sensitive skin. Her middle trembled with nerves and uncertainty. Why had he come today? Out of guilt? Was he checking on them to ease his conscience?

And why had he decided to stay in Verona Lake?

She curled her hands into fists to control their trembling. She mustn't fall prey to false hope. Drew's change of plans might have nothing to do with her.

He spoke first. "I just found out about the fire." His worried gaze swept her from head to toe as though looking for signs of injury. "Are you really all right?"

She nodded. "Yes. The paramedics checked us out. They gave Gracie some oxygen, but aside from that—" she broke off, her throat closing as she relived last night's terror. If anything had happened to Gracie...

Don't think about it. "We're fine."

"Thank God." He spoke the words like a prayer. Savannah's heart lurched when he took a step forward as though to give her a hug. When he stopped, her heart plummeted. From relief or disappointment?

"I feel so stupid," she said. "Forgetting to check the batteries in the smoke alarms." Her face burned with shame.

"Don't blame yourself."

But she did. If it hadn't been for Harley...

"Ty's been wonderful," she said hurriedly, changing the subject. "Letting us stay here until the inspectors tell us it's safe to go home."

He didn't speak, only stared at her as if assuring himself she wasn't an apparition, but really before him in flesh and blood. As the silence between them lengthened, she could only think to ask "You've really changed your mind about leaving? You seemed so sure of it before."

"I know it seems sudden. Like I can't make up my mind. But I never wanted to leave, not after meeting you and Gracie. There were things I didn't tell you." He let go a long breath. "My, uh, birth father suddenly showed up after years of...nothing. I thought he might want to reconnect, get to know me. Make amends for abandoning me and my mom. Turns out he has another family, and he was just sniffing around for a payout."

She felt the blood drain from her face. He must have been devastated. Without thinking, she took his hand. "Oh, Drew. I'm so sorry."

He shook his head. "It's like a stupid soap opera. He said if I didn't help him out, he'd go to the tabloids and make a big stink. I mean, I don't care what they say about me, but I didn't want them hurting people I care about. My family. You and Gracie."

People I care about. The phrase echoed in Savannah's ears.

"I know teachers have to watch their reputations," he went on. "People hold you to a higher standard. I didn't want anything to get you in trouble. Endanger your job. I thought if I cut ties, got out of town and stayed far away from you and Gracie—"

Savannah blinked. "You were trying to protect us?"

As her head spun, she squeezed his hand, using it to steady herself. It *did* sound like a soap opera. But he'd been thinking of her and Gracie. He'd meant well.

Still, a spark of resentment sizzled. "You couldn't have just been honest with me?"

His mouth twisted into something that was almost a smile. "My sister had a bone to pick with me on that score. She said I should have told you the truth. I'm sorry. I thought I was doing the right thing, not getting you involved. I messed up."

Her thoughts were as tangled as a basket full of wet laundry. "But you're here now. What's changed?"

"Frank—the old man—he backed down. Thanks to my kid brother. Yeah, I've got a brother I never knew existed. He's actually a decent guy."

One revelation after another left Savannah stunned. But one question gnawed at her—if this Frank guy hadn't backed down, would Drew even be here?

As though he read her mind, Drew told her "But I'd be here regardless. I'm not going away, Savannah. Not as long as you and Gracie are here. When I heard about the fire—" his voice broke and tears welled in his eyes. "I could have lost you…"

This time neither of them hesitated. He moved forward,

his arms open wide, and she stepped into his embrace. He held her as though to assure himself she was safe and whole. She held him longing for the dream that her loneliness might finally end.

But dreams were dangerous.

"Let me try again, Savannah," he murmured against her ear. "Please."

She wanted to trust him but wasn't sure she was brave enough. Loneliness was hard, but she'd gotten used to it. Risking her heart might mean getting it broken. She'd patched up its shards once before. She wasn't sure she could do it twice.

With her head on Drew's shoulder, she watched Harley trot over to Ty's cat and gently snuffle it. The cat blinked placidly, unperturbed.

Then the dog looked at her, a plea in his eyes. He picked up a neon-yellow tennis ball lying on the grass and carried it to her and Drew. They were still locked in their embrace. Very politely, he dropped the ball at their feet.

Drew held Savannah as if he never wanted to let her go. "He wants to play."

She clung to him. "I know."

Neither of them moved. The dog sat, waiting expectantly but patiently.

Funny Harley. Nothing got him down for long.

Brave Harley. Yes, he'd rescued them from the fire, but his courage ran even deeper than that. He'd been given away by people he loved and trusted, yet still he was brave enough to love again. To let go of the past and bond with a new family. He forgave scoldings and grumpy moods and grouchy tempers. He held no grudges. He greeted every day with happy woofs, a wagging tail, and a heart full of love.

Skeptics would roll their eyes and say he wasn't special at

all. That he was just a silly dog. But they'd be wrong. Harley wasn't silly. He was very wise.

He didn't live his life in fear.

And neither should I.

Gently freeing herself from Drew's embrace, she looked up at him and smiled. "Let's both try."

His expression softened. His eyes glistened with hope. "Yes?"

She nodded, feeling as light and tremulous as a bubble. "Yes."

Harley hopped to all fours, adding his *yes* with a glad huff.

Savannah laughed until Drew sealed her lips with a sweet kiss that sent tingles down to her toes. He withdrew with a gleam in his eye that promised more kisses, when they could be sure that a small face wasn't peeking at them through a patio door.

Gracie ran from the house, followed by Shelley and Ty, just as Drew picked up the ball and gave it a toss. "Go get it, Harley! Thatta boy!"

The dog raced to fetch the ball while Gracie clapped. "Yay, Harley!"

Harley picked up the ball where it landed and circled the yard with his prize. Then he trotted up to Savannah and deposited it at her feet. Love and gratitude flooded her as she stroked the soft fur between his ears. "You're such a good boy. Thank you."

Harley's tongue flapped in a joyous grin and his tail swished back and forth. *"You're welcome,"* she imagined him thinking. *"Now aren't you going to throw the ball?"*

And that was just what she did.

EPILOGUE

Harley

Today we are having a party and it is for me!

This morning the fire department gave me an award for being a Very Brave and Smart Dog. They put a fancy ribbon around my neck with a medal that says "K-9 Hero." I know because Gracie read it to me. The Fire Chief made a speech and a man took my picture while a TV lady talked to Mom and Gracie.

Now we are all at our friend Ty's house. My cat friends Boots and Zeno are here, too.

Zeno says "We're proud of you."

"Yeah, you did real good, Harley," Boots tells me. And hey! He said my real name and not Fuzz for Brains. I am so happy I give them each a big lick.

Outside I play Catch the Ball with Drew and Gracie. Boots decides to play, too. He runs and bops my nose with his paw when I try to get the ball. I chase him a little bit. Then he chases me. We are funny and make our people laugh.

Mom opens the patio door and calls "Lunch is ready, guys."

Boots scoots inside first while Mom holds the door. She looks confused but Ty laughs and says "It's okay. He's always here visiting my cat, anyway."

Zeno goes in, too. He never runs. He says it is undignified. Whatever that means.

I stop to pick up my ball and follow behind Drew and Gracie. My heart does a happy bounce when I see Drew take Mom's hand. My Gracie sees, too, and she gives me a smile because our secret plan is working.

I love my happy family of Gracie, Mom, and Aunt Shelley. I think we will be even happier when Drew becomes part of it, too.

Drew pats my head. Gracie gives me a hug.

Mom smiles at me. "Good boy, Harley."

My chest swells very proud and happy. At last I know the secret to being a Good Dog.

The secret is Love.

Thanks so much for reading **Pawsitively Love.** If you'd like to read more about the matchmaking pets in the *Fur-footed Friends* series, please check out these books:

Boots' story, **Purrfectly Matched**

A contemporary riff on **Puss in Boots** featuring a fake relationship, a cinnamon roll hero and a very snarky cat.

And Zeno's story, **A Purrfect Promise**

Shelley and Ty can't stand each other—or so it seems. But one smart cat sees through them both.

ALSO BY CHRISTIE LOGAN

The Billionaire Looks Back *(The Billionaire Pact, Book 1)*

A famous athlete turned billionaire. The woman he loved and left behind. When they meet again, will sparks re-ignite? Or will a long-kept secret tear them apart forever?

The Buttoned-Up Billionaire *(The Billionaire Pact, Book 2)*

He's a billionaire whose wealth and power were determined from birth. She's a free spirit whose life can fit in a rucksack. They should be adversaries...but can they look beyond their differences to find love?

The Billionaire's Big Risk *(The Billionaire Pact, Book 3)*

When the billionaire bad boy fell for the level-headed, risk-averse working girl, everyone said it couldn't last—and they were right. When a life-threatening accident forces them together again, will they get a second chance, or is love too big a risk to take?

A Real Christmas (Love in Applewood, Book 1)

He's a lonely man who hates Christmas. She's a struggling single mom. As they rediscover the magic of the holiday, will they also find love?

Dear Acquaintance (Love in Applewood, Book 2)

A divorcee who's turned her back on romance meets an open-hearted widower. Can a fake date lead to true love?

A Gentle Heart (Love in Applewood, Book 3)

An ambitious man chasing success. An innocent young woman looking for love. Will his need to get ahead at all costs mean breaking her gentle heart?

Star Spangled Second Chance (Love in Applewood, Book 4)

They were best friends before he left town without a word. Now he's back. Will her heart be broken again?

A Firefighter's Luck (Love in Applewood, Book 5)

A feisty single mom on her own. A firefighter with a rocky past. Can they lower their guard long enough to let love in?

Snowflake Kisses: Three Sweet Winter-Themed Romances (Love in Applewood, Books 1- 3)

As cozy as cuddling up near the fireplace with a cup of hot cocoa, these three sweet romances will warm your winter nights. Each is centered around a winter holiday.

Purrfectly Matched: A Sweet Romantic Comedy (Fur Footed Friends, Book 1)

A contemporary riff on **Puss in Boots** featuring a fake relationship, a cinnamon roll hero and a very snarky cat.

A Purrfect Promise: A Sweet Enemies to Lovers Romance (Fur Footed Friends, Book 2)

Shelley and Ty can't stand each other—or so it seems. But Zeno the cat sees through them both.

Pawsitively Love: A Sweet Single Mom Romance (Fur Footed Friends, Book 3)

Can a little girl and a big goofy dog help two lonely people fall in love?

ABOUT THE AUTHOR

Christie Logan writes sweet romance straight from the heart. She lives in upstate New York with too many pets, too many dust bunnies lurking under the bed, and too many plot bunnies bouncing around in her head. She thinks everyone deserves a happy ending and in her books, everyone gets one.

For more about her books, please visit her website: https://christielogan.com/

Would you like to learn more about Christie's upcoming releases and sales? **Sign up for her newsletter here**. You'll also receive a free read!

Made in United States
North Haven, CT
13 April 2022

18186624R00114